BBC
National
Short Story
Award 2018

with Cambridge University

First published in Great Britain in 2018 by Comma Press.
www.commapress.co.uk

'To Belong To' by Kerry Andrew © Kerry Andrew 2018

'Sudden Traveller' by Sarah Hall © Sarah Hall 2017,
first published by Audible

'Van Rensburg's Card' by Kiare Ladner © Kiare Ladner 2018

'The Sweet Sop' by Ingrid Persaud © Ingrid Persaud 2018,
first published by Granta Magazine

'The Minutes' by Nell Stevens © Nell Stevens 2018

A CIP catalogue record of this book is available
from the British Library.

ISBN 1-910974-41-2
ISBN-13 9781910974414
The publisher gratefully acknowledges the support
of Arts Council England.

Supported using public funding by
ARTS COUNCIL
ENGLAND

Set in Bembo 11/13
Printed and bound in Great Britain by Clays Ltd, Elcograf S.p.A

Contents

Introduction

Graham Greene once said something about short stories being necessarily more 'perfect' than novels. The latter, he argued, take a long time to complete, and so the author's character is changing all of the time during the composition. It is a different writer who finishes the book to the one who started it. The result is inconsistency, and a 'roughness to the work'. Short stories, in contrast, can be smooth, finished and (most importantly) consistent.

I have to say that – until the judging process for the 2018 BBC National Short Story Award with Cambridge University – I was no great advocate for, or even much sensible of, the virtue of consistency. I valued local touches in the prose coupled with big ideas: a piece of writing had to succeed at the level of the sentence, and do something significant on a broad scale. That made me happy enough.

Or so I thought. One of the many pleasures of reading so many short stories, and listening to the musings of my fellow judges, has been to make me think about what it is that makes a good piece of writing good. So often I was brought up by a comment from the judging panel – three of whom are professional writers; wielders of words with precision and purpose – about the accuracy of the prose. 'The point of view is not maintained', it was patiently explained, or 'the character would not think like that', or 'this contradicts what she felt the day before'. In other words, the judges were always advocates for consistency.

One of the greatest feelings a writer can have is the knowledge that their words are being read with care and sympathy. And I can assure those whose stories were judged this year that – in this panel of Sarah Howe, Benjamin Markovits, KJ Orr and Di Speirs – they found sympathetic, thoughtful, diligent and forensic readers. Writers also need to feel that their work is being rewarded; sadly that is so rarely the case in the current publishing industry. It is peculiarly pleasant to be involved in a process, at least, which will end in talented people getting unexpectedly paid. And all five stories presented here display signs of conspicuous talent.

'Sudden Traveller' by Sarah Hall is about grief and life. It tells the story of a woman nursing her child at the same time as she mourns the death of her mother. The opposition is there, stark and structural, at the beginning of the piece: 'You breastfeed the baby in the car, while your father and brother work in the cemetery.' Of course, that whole opposition – tomb and womb – is familiar in literary terms, but Hall wants us (and the second-person address of the story is particularly insistent) to reflect anew on the sensations of both birth and death. At the level of individual detail, the writing is especially rewarding, delving right down to 'the subterranean surgical thread they'd used to stitch you closed, its two blue beads'. And the mood is muted, like the 'unrelieved ache' of sorrow, but also contemplative, sensitive to the idea that life persists, both heedless to your loss (those mountains that 'will neither pity nor forgive you') and yet enabling you to measure and remember the life that has gone.

Hall's ability to render the reality of death in solid terms is matched by Ingrid Persaud's 'The Sweet Sop'. It marks the passing of another parent: Reggie, the absentee father of the narrator, Victor. Here, Victor's voice is the star. He speaks in a vibrant patois that commemorates the moments of connection with his Dad through the sweet food they shared: 'This secret chocolate handover was our special sin. Everybody know that a little secret-sinning sweet too bad. If you don't agree I know you lying through your teeth.'

As the two men share the chocolate, so their relationship comes to represent an inversion of the parent–child dependency, and the pain of the father's earlier neglect is finally soothed. As with 'Sudden Traveller', the story looks ahead to a time when grief will eventually soften, like chocolate.

Another innocuous daily item is at the centre of 'Van Rensburg's Card' by Kiare Ladner: a note of consolation given to Greta on the death of her husband. Eighteen months after receiving it, Greta's life is a minor maelstrom of loneliness and awkwardness: she has a distant relationship with her daughter Nikki, who has moved to another country, and become unreceptive. Greta's experiences in a shopping centre – full of mishaps and miscalculations – are deftly offered as examples of the low-key sadness in her life. Should she accept the sympathy of a stranger? Is any human connection better than none at all?

The value of community, emphasised by contrast in Ladner's story, is the heroic centrepiece to Kerry Andrew's 'To Belong To', which begins with contemplation of suicide on an isolated Scottish isle. The central figure – like many of the characters in this list – is affected by grief, damaged by life: he 'imagines himself broken on the rocks on the north side, thinks of other broken things, of strip lights and phone calls, and he sleeps again, the waves of the wind smoothing him into nothing'. This is a tale about the power of people to be repaired, the salutary effect of companionship and friendship, a narrative of 'bright, fresh days' amid so much surrounding gloom. It tells us of the charming potential of existence, and is charmingly written to boot.

That concept of connection is present in 'The Minutes' by Nell Stevens, written as an address to an unnamed lover, a professor, by a young woman involved in protesting against the gentrification of an area, and demolition of a housing block. There is satire of the good-natured pretentiousness of students using conceptual art to embody their objection ('Imagine what it would look like if, when the demolition began, the bricks went up instead of down'), but also the familiar plangency of a difficult love story that teeters around tragedy.

These are just snapshots of the stories you are about to read, and which we spent an enjoyable, achingly hot summer debating. F. Scott Fitzgerald once exhorted writers to 'find the key emotion; this may be all you need to know to find your short story'. I think my fellow judges demanded more, actually, when finding their favourites. Emotion, of course, is important, and it is striking how many pivot around the wrenching response to loss. But we also demanded control and cohesion, the firm grip of the author upon their chosen material. The result is these five stories you now have in front of you. You are in safe hands, I promise.

Stig Abell
London, 2018

To Belong To

Kerry Andrew

THIS IS A GOOD place to die.

He stands at the edge. The height sends the hangover lurching to his stomach. The closeness of toes to air.

Below, the sea is bladed, black. A thousand fulmars stipple the cliffs either side of him, their cries a blur. On the lowest rocks, a little way out, are the thicker brushstrokes of seals, resting.

There had been talk of hearing their song, but if it is there, it is blunted by the wind.

He curls his toes. The ground curves, falls away gently, almost inviting it.

There will be a short moment of great pain. His head might catch on a rock. His back break.

But once he has made the decision to jump, he will have to take whatever comes.

One movement. A footstep, into nothing.

In the sea, by the seal rocks, there is a small

spot, bobbing. A lone adventurer perhaps, going further out to find the fish.

Another breath or two, to listen for the singing.

He closes his eyes, holds his arms out. The Angel of the North, transported to the outer edge of the country. He stands as still as he is able.

When he opens his eyes again, the spot has moved past the others, towards the cliffs.

He watches, wind pummelling the length of his arms.

In the shallows, it rises, and is not a seal. Long slabs of flesh, dark at the ends. The woman stands for a moment, looking back out to sea, and he thinks he hears something, words or a melody. Then she is turning, walking the few steps over the paler stones to a strung ladder that he had not noticed, tucked in at the bottom of the rocks. His eyes trace the journey that she must take, move just ahead of her as she scrambles over turf and quickly crosses two unsecured planks of wood. A rope, glinting silver, zigzags up the cliff and she ascends, once or twice leaning outwards, very close to the edge.

She disappears for a moment in the fold of the hill and he waits, his eyes on the sodden green line where she must appear. He puts his arms by his sides.

A fulmar passes at head height. He can see the architecture of its beak.

There.

She walks towards him, clothed now. Sports leggings, a fleece. The gloves and socks she was wearing gone. Her hair is mostly slicked back, a short cap of it, glints of blue or green, almost mineral. Her arms are folded, shoulders hunched. She keeps walking towards him and for a second he wonders if he *has* jumped, that his body lies dismantled on the stones, before she stops right next to him.

Push me, he thinks.

She stares up at him. Hard, brown eyes. 'Come on,' she says, before striding past.

And he does.

★

The woman's house is a white bungalow at the other end of the island, amongst a scatter of cottages. She hadn't said anything in the car, tapping two fingers on the steering wheel.

'Did you come on the cruise ship?' She nibbles at the scone that she has already called dry. Her teeth are small and slightly rounded. Her tomboyish hair has dried, revealed itself as aegean blue. It has emerged from the sea later than her.

He shakes his head. Words are difficult, as if they have to be re-shaped into something recognisable. 'Bird Obs.'

'*Obvs,*' she says, and there is a crooked grin. 'Didn't they all go back today?'

He nods.

'Obvs,' she says again, very quietly and more deliberately, and looks at him. The underside of one eye creases. 'Eat,' she says. Nods at the plate.

His stomach feels complicated, not ready to consume again. He looks at the scone in his hand.

'Or not,' she says.

★

She is called Anna. She lives alone in the little cottage and she is from Estonia. 'I do not belong to here,' she says, and winks. 'Just like you.'

She only asks questions that are practical and of the present, though her looks are acute. She leaves him sitting at the table by the window while she stacks things in the kitchen.

The field sweeps up from the house, the long grass sleek and full of movement. Sheep have their heads down as they eat and there is a flock of golden plover. A church sits on top of the low hill, its tower stark against the white sky.

The plovers suddenly take flight, a large bird amongst them. He almost instinctively reaches for binoculars at his chest, before remembering that he left everything in his sports bag, tucked behind a rock not far from the North Quay.

Clothes. Passport. Watch. Wallet. He'd taken out the photo of her, and put it back in again.

Instead he watches the trajectory of the bird of prey, its calm, ominous dance as it turns and follows them. A hen harrier, perhaps, rare for Shetland. He waits for it to come back.

It has got late. He has not moved from his chair, and he is not sure if he is alone in the house. It is quiet.

He gets up and passes through the house, listening. The wind has risen, shouldering itself against the walls. The corridor opens onto different rooms – a living room, bathroom, a bedroom in disarray, clothes tossed onto the floor. There is a single lamp on at the far end of the house, and he knocks on the door, pushes it open an inch.

A single room, a quilt with a Scandinavian pattern, neatly tucked. Two books on the pillow.

'It's yours,' Anna says behind him, her coat on and keys in her hand. 'You'll stay tonight.'

*

He sleeps. He sleeps soundly, his body weighted. He wakes in a panic and imagines himself broken on the rocks on the north side, thinks of other broken things, of strip lights and phone calls, and he sleeps again, the waves of the wind smoothing him into nothing.

★

In the morning, there is an all-consuming fog. He cannot see the end of the field.

'You're not going anywhere,' says Anna, her arms wrapped around her, staring out of the window. It is hard to tell exactly what she means.

Something moves out there. Low shadows, only just tangible. 'Are they yours?'

'Yeah,' she says, and sniffs. 'Pain in the arse.'

He walks in the fog. He walks the length of the island, which is not far, though it feels unknowable in this weather. As if it is hiding its edges from him.

'Have a nice time,' Anna had said, and it had sounded almost like a challenge. 'Lasagne later.'

He passes the mist nets, the unnerving structures of wood and nylon mesh. Some concrete blocks with gaping windows, their use unclear. He nears the North Light but is afraid, as if the cliff might crumble away beneath him.

There is movement over his head, a bird. The great skuas are protecting their eggs, but there is something thuggish about them. It is said that they will pretend to be injured on the path, to lure people closer. 'Vindictive little shitbags,' Josie would have said, delightedly appalled. 'Come and have a go if you think you're hard enough.'

He gets lost on the boggy hillside. Another skua comes down, very close. He walks fast, comes across a small skeleton, and another, black, torn. He thinks it is her and almost throws up.

He sees a small triangle of something that looks like pottery and puts it in his palm. Navy-blue and tangerine. There are more, further off. It is a puffin graveyard.

On his way back, he sits in the kirk, looking up at the fruit pastille colours of the stained glass and words to commemorate an islander. *Awaiting the going down of the sun to be joined again in Paradise.*

The chill in his bones feels permanent.

Why is it capitalised? The letters of that word begin to tease apart until they are individually suspended, runic.

There is no Paradise for her.

★

A day passes. The fog remains. He does not see Anna much. There is food left on the kitchen counter for him, notes. He sits quietly in the house, hands around a mug. It is beyond generous that she has let him stay.

He knows that he must book a plane seat, and that he should have done it much in advance, though the weather makes it impossible for now. There is the option of the boat, two and half hours to the mainland.

Instead, he walks to the outskirts of the fog. He covers all of the roads, and begins to take paths to see where they lead. He is seen by others, at a distance. Wondered about. They revisit the old ghost stories, and wonder if they can place him within them.

At Anna's, they eat simply, food from the polytunnel at the back of the house. Onions, carrots, potatoes. Mackerel, caught and smoked by a neighbour. Anna talks about her sheep, points to them through the window. She has given them the names of silent film stars. He thinks, *I will get through the next hour, and the next one.*

He walks down to the southern beach and watches a seal curve itself on a rock, head and tail raised.

He does not book the plane. He does not take the ferry.

He mentions to Anna that he is quite good with cars, and she immediately stands, demands that he follow her outside, lifts the bonnet. He spends a day working on it, though it needs a new fan belt in truth, and touches the dents up, sprays WD-40 on the spark-plugs. She looks at him as if he's done something magical.

★

The fog lifts. The island is revealed again.

He begins to have places he returns to. The large rock with the natural seat at the southern beach, boots getting wet if the tide has come in too far. The brute concrete squares of the old radar station. The teetering view where the water churns and it is said there was a great shipwreck. The chapel, smaller than the kirk and less blameful.

He does not book a plane, or take the ferry.

He walks. Is greeted, understatedly. Begins to respond.

★

Anna knows some of the stories of the wrecks, rattling them off as if to a tourist. The Viking longship, and the boat from the Spanish Armada,

300 men coming ashore and their legacy in the dark eyes and hair of some of the locals. 'You cannot escape us bloody foreigners,' she says.

She has dived down to them, found musket balls. The flat-edged ones were fired by the English. 'The Spanish would press-gang you and let you *gang* home,' she says. 'The English would press-gang you and never let you return.'

She wiggles her fingers, her face full of mock suspense.

'*Dun dun dunnnn.*'

Anna is more interested in shells, stones. The island doesn't stop at the door but moves through the house. She shows him a large scallop, a tortoiseshell limpet, the degraded vertebra of a minke whale. She gives him a round, pink rock, its texture mottled and woollen-looking.

He cradles it.

It is the size and weight of a newborn's skull.

★

He watches a man build boats, his hair the same blonde as the wood. Watches the shape of it come, and how it echoes water.

He helps Anna with the leak in her shower pipe. The unyielding radiator. The fan above the oven. She asks him to look at paint colours on the internet. She jokes that the house will be a different house after he has left.

They eat lobster, barley porridge. Lamb.

He hears how people born on the island leave to find work in Bergen, Aberdeen, London, and how some return. Others have never lived anywhere else. He learns that 'to belong to' means 'to come from'.

Two men stand with him, talk of how small islands have been understood, these last decades, supported. 'They think we are all like them, bloody island mentality,' the older man says.

Someone has heard about Anna's car. Asks him to look at theirs. He spends an afternoon with oil on his hands, the sun striping his forehead.

★

No one asks why he is still here. Perhaps it is spoken of, quietly, by the woman who runs the shop, or the ferry-worker who lives in the sheltered housing.

The man who didn't leave. He imagines talk of him travelling across the lower half of the island, a wren's flight.

★

He begins to know everyone's names. It is not hard. There are only so many here. He begins to understand the families, some stretching back several hundred years, others very new. There is a Venezuelan woman, a Romanian nurse. There are those from mainland Scotland who came on a holiday in their twenties and remain fifty years later. There is a couple that came on a whim, having only known each other a few months, and there is a man from upstate New York who runs a bed and breakfast.

Steven takes him out on his fishing boat, and hardly speaks, except to explain about the fishing line and that he has rescued sailors more than once, their boats dashed to pieces by the next morning.

He looks at the island from the sea, and how it speaks differently. How whole it is.

Steven pulls up three mackerel, evenly-striped and flapping. Later, there's a cod, imperious in death, smudges of amber on its tail.

Sandeels are partly used as bait and kept in a coolbox. They shift and hustle, iridescent. He holds one in his hand, remembers the umbilical cord, how monstrous it looked. Josie, and the long silence before she began to cry.

★

There are other ghosts here. Steven tells a story of two men and a black dog seen one night, who no one knew and did not see again. The next morning, the long masts of a shipwrecked schooner were spotted offshore.

*

He is taken to dinner. He listens to an argument over politics, the woman laughing and saying she is only playing devil's advocate, that she isn't an idiot. Anna talking of large-scale protests and making banners.

The rain comes, and the evening is cut short. He is enlisted to help with the hay bales.

*

On the southern beach, he comes across two girls, squatting down with their fingers in the sand and stone. He has seen them before – there are only three children on the island, the older ones boarding on the mainland. One girl likes to jump on the trampoline in her garden.

The other lives at the Bird Obs and is often holding the hand of her smaller sibling, both in wellies.

They are looking for cowrie shells but have

not seen any. They show him their findings: a limpet shell, jam-coloured seaweed dried onto it in an attractive pattern; a speckled sea urchin that is tiny even on the pad of the seven-year-old's forefinger; a stone with an askew smile. The older girl has an American accent.

He looks out to sea, still crouched down.

They ask him if he wants to see something secret. He looks at them.

They wander ahead, further along the stones. He follows. Past a small promontory in the cliff, there is a cleft of rock partly covered in dense, impossibly green moss, grass, ferns. On a treeless island, it is almost embarrassingly fertile. As if the rock has opened its hands, conjured something miraculous.

'Isn't it beautiful?' says one of the girls. 'Hardly anyone knows it's here. Everywhere else is so barren, and then look.'

The three of them stare at it.

At Anna's that evening, he looks at the detailed, hand-drawn map that is sold by the Bird Obs.

On an island where every rock, geo, rivvie and head is named, the cleft is a wordless place.

*

Anna paints. She likes to paint the things she finds, places them in rows according to shape and size and colour. Or she arranges them differently, one of every type of object – driftwood, queen scallop, sea-glass. She sits with her oil-lamp on and one of her CDs playing, her shoulders hooked over her work. The paintings dry on a shelf above a radiator, the paper rising at the edges, crisp.

She puts the paintbrush in the dirty-water jar. Narrows her eyes at him. 'It's time,' she says. 'I'm going to do you.'

An hour later, she stands and holds the stiff paper for him to see.

He looks at this water-version of himself, the unkempt hair and stubble. The grey eyes. It is imperfect.

'Is that me?' he says.

'It's you,' she says. 'Or near enough.'

★

Anna is changeable. Often crabby in the mornings, sleep in her eyes, her cardigan wrapped round her, shuffling around in two pairs of knitted socks. Or suddenly surging with energy, the house unable to contain her. He hears her singing English pop songs a little tunelessly, the words not quite right.

She sits in the corner chair, finishing a hat. The word is *finishing* and not knitting, because she is not yet good enough to knit from scratch, she says, rolling her eyes. Another woman designs them. This one is from the wool of the island's sheep, un-dyed. White, grey, black, brown. The yarn has been hand-spun by Steven on the spinning-wheel he made himself.

He hears her on the phone to her mother, the swish and wry musicality of her native tongue. It is not so different from the accent here.

He walks into the bathroom to find her wrapping herself in a towel. His apology is overdone and she just watches him, grinning.

One night, they share a bottle of wine and she plays him boisterous Hungarian jazz and gypsy punk.

She dances around the room, before sitting astride his thighs.

'I can't,' he says. His mouth is dry.

She watches him, the curl of her lip slowly fading, and she shrugs. 'Suit yourself, *mu nukker poiss.*'

*

The phone rings. It rings a lot here – there is barely any mobile reception on the island. He has not thought to ring anyone.

Anna tucks the phone into her shoulder, as she always does, folds her arms.

'Right,' she says as she puts it down. 'To the Annamobile.'

They go in the car, stopping less than half a mile away. There is a cluster of people on the cliff, wax jackets and telescopes. James, the ferry skipper, hands him some binoculars, points.

Out on the sea, a lone ring-necked duck is gently buoyed. A dark, slightly tufted head and cream flanks. It is North American and has not been seen here since the 1970s, James says. It is nicknamed a *lifer* – a species you might only see once in your life.

The water has become almost completely still. It has the texture of a hospital blanket.

'If you hadn't been here, you wouldn't have seen it ever,' says Anna. 'Bet your lifer.'

★

He goes to the place where he left his bag. It is not there.

He walks to the Bird Obs, asks. A volunteer, perhaps one who has only been here a couple of weeks, comes back out with it, uninterested. Everything is still in it.

As twilight finally comes, he sits on his southern beach rock and thinks of his child. Of her tiny hands. Of how they didn't name her.

The sun joins the sea.

He thinks of his girlfriend, silent with grief, fragmented, going back to the other side of the world.

*

Some musicians come from London and play a concert. Their arrival brings a succession of *given days*, days without wind. Everyone on the island packs into the community hall. It hums with their smells. With warmth. A woman touches her cello as if it is a lover who is leaving her, her eyes closed, full of concentration.

The piece was written by a composer in a prisoner-of-war camp in 1941, and premiered there on inferior instruments. Listened to by four hundred prisoners and guards. A piece infused with birdsong, angels, heaven.

A senior man from the island stands. Everyone listens as he speaks of the war, and of a Scotsman captured on Crete, who dreamed of building a bird observatory on the island while a prisoner for two and a half years in Germany. There are deep nods.

Afterwards, he feels shattered. Drinks are served, the talk high and loud, and he hovers in the corner, watching the cellist, wondering where that light and anguish has gone, whether it has been packed away with the instrument in its case.

Anna puts her hand on his back. 'Want to come bird?'

He looks at her.

'The stormies are here,' she says.

★

It is the clearest of nights. The Milky Way is capacious, and he can see the flat disc of the Pleiades. There is a strange lightness to the clouds on the northern horizon.

At the Bird Obs, a high-pitched burbling sound curls in the air. An electronic rendering of storm petrels. Two staffers, torches on their hard hats, wait by the funnel trap.

The office feels more sacred to him than the chapel, tiny and gently illuminated. He and Anna, the American girl and her father stand still as a staffer hangs up two small, soft bags, their contents shifting and rustling. The man brings out a bird, cradling the body, its neck loosely circled by his thumb and forefinger. It stills.

The storm petrel is wind-honed and the colour of coal dust, apart from a white bar above its tail. A hard, bright eye. The staffer tightens a new silver ring around its ankle and explains how far north they might have come from on their way to West Africa, Namibia. He holds the bird upright, spreads its long, fine-tipped wing for them all to see, before putting the bird back into its bag.

Anna looks at him. 'Come on,' she says, with the same brusque simplicity as that first time on the cliff.

They go back outside and he feels as if he is walking into a ceremony, a ritual that he is afraid of. The staffer is murmuring to the American girl a little further away. It is so dark that he does not understand what is to happen.

'Do this,' Anna says, and puts her hands out in front of her.

He does so, and waits. Hands cupped, looking at the astonishing spread of stars.

The staffer is next to him. 'OK?' he says.

'Yes.'

A bird is placed into his palms. Even though his hands are in front of his torso, he cannot see it. The storm petrel is impossibly light and vibrates like a small electrical toy. He feels its utter terror, its resilience, the power of this long-distance traveller. There is something communicated, something more fiercely concentrated than words.

He names his child, silently, a name only for him, rising up with the bird as it suddenly vanishes from his hands, the darkness of the bird into the darkness of the night.

He remains still, his hands in their nest-shape. A half-moon lifts, honey-coloured and awkward, as if cut out and elevated by puppeteers.

'That's not supposed to be there at this time of year,' says Anna, frowning.

*

Bright, fresh days. One of the four cows on the island is let loose, and no one owns up to it.

Anna's hair loses its tropical colour, matches the cool, early autumn skies. She swims. He runs.

He helps round up the sheep, cups their chins as the drench gun is shoved in, begins to know Clara Bow from Louise Brooks.

They go to a party. There is whisky, beef stew, vegetables from the garden. Mid-century jazz is played and *guyzing* wigs are tried on months early to screeches, howls. One of the young women knits in a corner. There is a mention of a name he has not heard before, and he sees how everyone quietens, looks at their drinks, toasts her, and how the conversation is not the same after that.

Steven has brought his accordion and his knotted hands do not seem to hamper him. Another plays fiddle, and a woman sings and plays guitar.

A man tells a story about a tall figure seen one New Year's Eve, going up to a house but never arriving. 'About your height,' he says, looking over, and everyone laughs gently.

He looks at his drink, smiles, thinks, *I am a ghost, but I am not that one.*

★

They walk back along the road, the southern lighthouse's beam passing over at intervals, and otherwise a profound sense of night. No stars. Anna leans into him, the drink making her sparkle, and he thinks, *you're a madwoman. God.*

On the air comes an eerie, hollowing sound – or many sounds, distant and threading tightly together. An ululation, not quite graspable.

Seals, singing.

Anna throws her head back. A small, spiralling wail. The sound a child makes to represent a ghost. She stops, looks over at him and laughs, loudly, puckishly.

That night, he knocks on her bedroom door. She is still a little drunk, laughing as she pretends to be sexy, pulling her lip down with her finger, biting it, but it arouses him nonetheless.

She has a tattoo of a dolphin on her hip, an old one that she talks about dismissively.

She sits on top of him, pushes at his thighs, shoving until she is comfortable, appearing deep in thought. And then her eyes are on him, her face close, and she says, 'Go on, then.'

Afterwards, they listen to the birdfeeder being knocked against the window by the wind.

'Do you want me to go?' he says.

'Why do you think that?'

'I've been here too long.'

'Do you mean that?' She stares at him, props herself up on an elbow. She looks angry. 'Do you?'

'I don't know.'

She lies back down. Kicks his calf, lightly. 'Don't go until you know.'

*

The island is battered by storms, the sea apocalyptic. Anna shaves her head. There is a craving for stodgy food, the TV. A craving to leave, too, for trees, for more than the same faces over and over.

He volunteers to take the sheep to be sold on the mainland. The boat rolls deeply and excrement slops over his wellies. The animals are obtuse and terrified, and he has to watch them to make sure they do not simply stop breathing.

The mainland is startling – the longer roads, the signs, the shops. He sits alone in the pub, listening to the Norwegian oil workers, the first pint he has had in his hand since last summer.

He feels light-headed, shaky. He feels the pull of the island.

*

He returns. The darkness tightens around them, long months of it, before light begins to embrace the island again.

He helps with the lambing, slick bodies coming out into his arms. One is stillborn and Anna watches him, carefully.

It is matted, bloody, as limp as an ancient teddy bear.

He wipes its mouth, passes it on.

*

He visits the lush secret hollow on the southern beach. The two girls who are sisters hop after him.

He tells them he has a name for it, and they test it on their tongue, and approve.

They tell Anna when they all come back in and she says yes, it is a good name, and she gives them a piece of chocolate each, and pops one in his mouth, too. Calls him *kullake*.

*

A year has passed. The fog is here again, nudging and close. He pushes through it to the north end of the island, and walks until his toes meet the curve where the cliff begins to slide forward.

He is going to the mainland tomorrow to pick up supplies – spices, boots, a new fan belt now that Anna's car has surrendered.

The fog peels away. The brightness of the North Light and the brightness of the sea.

He puts his arms out. Closes his eyes.

This is a good place to die.

Sudden Traveller

Sarah Hall

YOU BREASTFEED THE BABY in the car, while your
father and brother work in the cemetery. They
are clearing the drains of leaves and silt, so your
mother can be buried. November storms have
brought more rain than the valley has ever seen.
The iron gates of the graveyard are half gone, the
residents of the lower-lying graves are being
made moist again. Water trickles under the car's
wheels. The river has become a lake; it has
breached the banks, spanned the valley's sides.
And still the uplands weep. On the radio they
have been talking about rescue squads, helicopters,
emergency centres in sports parks and village
halls. The army is bringing sand. They have been
comparing measurements from the last one
hundred years. The surface of the floodwater is
decorated with thousands of rings as the rain
comes down.

Inside the car is absolute stillness. When he is finished, the baby sleeps against your side. There are only two small feeds a day now. His mouth has become a perfect tool and you no longer have any marked sensation, no tingling, no pressure across the chest wall as the milk lets down. His mouth remains slightly open, his cheeks flushed. There are bright veins in his eyelids, like light filaments in leaves. He rests heavily against you, hot, breathing softly, like a small machine, an extra organ worn outside the body. You could try to place him carefully on the front seat, under a blanket, get out and help clear the leaves. You would like to feel the cold air against your face and hands as it streams over the mountains. You would like to work with the men. But you dare not move. If the baby senses a temperature change, he will wake, he will want more of you. You could wear him in the sling to work, but the rain keeps coming, slanted, determined to find everything.

You sit in the car, watching reefs of cloud blow across the valley, watching the trees bow and lean and let go of their last leaves, hearing the occasional lost call between your father and brother, and feeling the infant heat against your side. So often it is like this – suspension from the world. Waiting to rejoin. Nobody warned you about this part. The baby is some kind of axis. He is a fixed point in time, though he grows every day, fingers lengthening, face passing through echoes of all your relatives, and the other relatives, heart chambers expanding, blood reproducing. It is like holding a star in your arms. A radiant new thing, whose existence was unimagined before it was discovered, illuminating so many zones, and already passing. All stories begin and end with him. All the moments of your life, all its meanings and dimensions, seem to lead to him and from him.

In the hospital, he played with the plastic identity bracelet the nurse gave him, identical to the one your mother was wearing. He threw it on the floor and everyone, even the consultant, picked it up and gave it back, laughing. No one could resist such a game. Joy in the midst of trauma; such a welcome relief. *Should we write his name on it,* a nurse asked. *No, no,* you said. *Absolutely not.* To do so would have been macabre, you thought. Then again, you kept the tiny one from his birth in a box of medical mementos — the woollen hat they put on him, despite the heat of July, despite his raw scalp, the subterranean surgical thread they'd used to stitch you closed, its two blue beads. Perhaps it was occult to have done so. The power of artefacts, like a ritualistic horde. Perhaps in keeping such items, you have created a dark charge.

Good as gold, the nurses said as he played on the ward floor. He smiled at the ladies in their beds, ladies of ruin, gowned, chronically pained, with systems in shut down, embarrassed by their smells. You could see his effect, like tonic, for them. They remembered their own children and their lined faces softened. *What a poppet,* they said. *Bonnie lad, you've come to see your granmammy.* He watched your mother jerk under the white sheet, too young, of course, to understand. It might have seemed like a silly game. You took him outside when the nurses changed her pads; you knew she would want that privacy. You walked him on your feet down the corridor, holding his wrists, his operator, his avatar. You bought coffee for everyone in the hospital café – your dad, brother, even your niece and nephew were drinking it – then came back to take your place at the vigil.

The nurses were all talking about death around her bed, casually, the normalness of dying, and at first you were horrified, you wanted to tell them to stop it, shut up, it would frighten your mother to hear such things. Then you began to see they were, in fact, comforting her, better than you could. Dying: like having a wash, like stirring sugar into tea, or laying out cutlery. It was the first instruction – of what would become a vital list of instructions – in bringing the experience close, the importance of feeling its brush, coolly against your skin.

You sat your son on your mother's bed, keeping him away from the intravenous pump pushing morphine. Enough morphine to relieve, but not to render insensate, yet – let her be conscious for the goodbyes. They had removed the feeding tubes, which was also an act of kindness, no matter how counter-intuitive. The baby reached for the dish and the sponge with which you had been wetting her dry mouth. He reached for your mother's twitching fingers. Everything in her was breaking down. They told you some part of her would know what was going on in the room around her, she would be able to hear at least and at last, and yes, you think she did near. Your son's name was the only word she could say properly, though she was trying and trying to talk, hoarsely, making no sense. When you held him close, and put her hand on his head, on that beautiful drift of hair above his neck, her eyes focused for a moment, on you, on him. She said, *Hello* –

The ward was full. The hospital was full. Winter, the season of infection, of brutalisation of the weak and the old. Within half a day, the nurses had found her – through some complicated political subterfuge, something they do not teach during medical education – a private room. Less than 48 hours, the consultant had said, once they'd admitted her and run tests. You forget exactly who broke that piece of news – your dad, your brother, one of the doctors, maybe. You were already en route to the hospital, halfway up the motorway, on speakerphone. The night before, she'd fallen out of bed, and your father and neighbour – a first responder – could not get her back up and in, though she weighed, by then, very little. You knew it was not good. You had been keeping, in fact, a small overnight bag under your bed, ready. *Thank you,* you said, to whichever green-winged angel told you, *thank you for letting me know.* You did not pull over into a layby or service station, though you were advised to pull over, to sit quietly for half an hour, to have a cup of strong tea, maybe call someone to comfort you. Who idles after such news? Instead, you gripped the steering wheel, accelerated up to 90mph, took the outer lane, and switched on the wipers. The baby slept in his tilted seat. There were already weather warnings, talk of road closures, diversions. There were clouds the colour of iron ahead of you.

It is now you are sitting quietly, in the little pull-off beside the village cemetery, with water surrounding the car, in twilight-hour light, though it is eleven fifteen in the morning. It has been eleven fifteen for much longer than a minute, you are sure. The clock does not move. The baby burns against your ribs, emitting, absorbing. Now there is time to sit, all the time in the world, and no more time. Time: the most un-relatable concept. To have come to depend on it, to have defined everything by it: so foolish. If you were to step off this planet, you would not need such identification; everything would bend and fold and repeat, or simply release. You would have no age. You would cease to be complete in status. What, you wonder, does that mean for the self? Many selves, all in existence at once? That's a story you have heard, some kind of scientific proposition you don't quite understand, though the idea seems right. And the truth is, where you are now, caught inside the storm, travelling in its eye, so tired, so undefined, so lost, you could almost be reached by these other yous, inhabited, comforted, replaced.

Your brother carries a bag of wet leaves out of the cemetery. His coat is stained, his trousers soaked to the thigh. He looks towards the car, doesn't smile, which is unusual but understandable. He and his wife and their kids are staying at your parents' house. Your father's house. You are too. The house where you were raised, and in which your mum and dad lived for nearly fifty years. All of you, over the last week, have been driving to and from the hospital, dozing in the chairs, bringing supplies. Only your father remained in full attendance, requesting clothes and his medication. The nurses were kind about suspending the restriction of visiting hours, you must remember to write to them in appreciation, do something for them, send them a set of tea cups, perhaps, they drink so much tea. You should make a list of things to do, people to thank.

Tell me when, your brother had said to your dad the last night at the hospital, as he was leaving, *tell me to come and I'll get there in time.* The hospital is nearly an hour's drive away, in the day, slow country roads, then steep northern motorway. Not exactly a swift journey. But at night, at night the north has other dimensions. The badlands emerge. Empty roads, shining like dark wounds through the mountains. Everything becomes more rapid, everything warps with momentum. Like the body's shadow systems, the ascendency of a virus, perhaps. You almost believe he would have got there. Four a.m. was when her breathing finally changed. But your brother was so worn out he slept and didn't hear the phone ringing. He didn't pick up the message, your father's anguished plea: *Come now.* A neighbour knocking on the door broke the news in the morning, and then your brother went out on the moor with the dogs and nobody knows what came next, but the dogs made their own way home. The stress, driving to and from her bedside, being husband and father, and a London worker, being a son losing a mother, had exhausted him. He will not forgive himself, you can see it written throughout him, and in the way his body moves between the graves. Penance. Hard labour. He wanted so badly to be there in that final moment.

You did not want to be there. You were afraid of that last inhalation, its lack of echo. You did not want to see the door close. You wanted those dry, wood-tongued breaths to go on and on, selfishly, fearfully, even though, when you had the room to yourself, you told her it was OK to go, you told her you and the others would be OK. *Just sleep, Mum.*

But you went to the morgue. You stood and you looked. She was so altered she seemed like another substance, not flesh. She looked like an image in the only dream you would ever have from then on. Why did you go? You've asked yourself. Because you had to see, to be sure of something. Your brother did not come into that back room. He sat with your niece and nephew and drank exceptionally well-made coffee with the morticians, allowed them to steward him, even to humour him, so good were they at their service, those two blue-robed, placid gladiators – you must write to them too. He didn't want to see her corpse. Each in their own wisdom; where the very face of death is concerned. Your brother's wife came in with you. *I don't think I can touch her,* you said, and you handed over a pair of little socks belonging to your son, and your brother's wife gently tucked them into your mum's hand, she who never considered herself brave, who exemplified, in that moment, all concept of bravery and kindness.

Your brother dumps the bag and goes back into the cemetery. You watch him through the bars of the gates. He rakes the leaves. He kicks at the blockages with his heel. He sweeps water down the culverts. He would climb into the sky if he could and hammer shut the clouds, command the rain to stop like some demented prophet. You could go to him and say: *She wouldn't have wanted us there. She spent her whole life making sure we would be spared such things.* Later you will say it to him, after the funeral.

The baby sleeps. That is his only commitment. You have not really slept for several days. The undertakers – who are, like the morticians, extraordinary, benign beings, who move through the darkest realms with a kind of grace and levity you can't fathom – have told you this is usual for the bereaved. Too much adrenalin has been dispensed into the body. Unusual psychological events need to be processed. All that survivalist caffeine has stoked you up too high. You are so tired there are moments you are not sure if you are awake anymore. It feels like those early newborn days, the fugue state of new motherhood, when the baby was in a separate plastic cot at your bedside. Your body had dumped out far too much of its red content. There was no involution yet, they couldn't stop the bleeding and chemicals were being used to shrink the womb. There was talk of a transfusion. You couldn't stand up to lift him, so from time to time he was being handed to you, then put back in the cot. There was no milk. The trauma of surgery had arrested it, or your body had just gone haywire. They were giving him formula to keep the weight on. His fontanel looked depressed. A wasp had come into the room and kept landing near his feet. Your eyes would simply not close. On the third night, you finally did sleep and there was a terrible dream. It was predominantly kinetic, like a falling dream, except you didn't wake suddenly from the sensation. You weren't falling. This dream was like an explosion in your core. Your atoms were blown apart and those pieces were drawn with tremendous force outwards and outwards, into the hospital room, into the sky, into black space and whatever lies at the furthest reaches, un-endingness, emptiness. It was exactly the kind of body shock that occurs after such deprivation, even after torture, you've read. But that doesn't alter the truth of the dream. After you'd come round, crying, hitting the alarm on the bed, you interpreted it in only one way. Transposition. The baby had come, and you would go, the universe was telling you. It was the most scared you've ever felt.

Two months later, the diagnosis came. Your mother had had backache for a while, since before you gave birth. She couldn't hold the baby either, though she tried several times and had to put him down. She was booked in for X-rays, then MRIs. You were visiting your parents at the time. They arrived home from the consultation and you saw their faces and knew what was coming. On the scans were shadows in the lungs and spine. The liver. Glands. Not yet the brain. Smoker. Decades of smoke.

It was early autumn, gilded, the gorse was going wild, so fragrant it was like another country, those long shadows running up and down the fells, quartering the fields, warm enough to swim in the river if you'd been the child you once were, river-child, still bright in the evening when you walked the lanes, the baby in the sling in front of you, your abdomen still aching from the section. With therapy, there would be a year, a little more, a little less, the statistics showed. It was a very standard, very predictable cancer. Everyone should prepare, though how to prepare can never be clear. *Ask questions,* friends said. *Spend time. Take videos. Listen to stories.* Stories. There was, of course, the ongoing joy of the baby for your mother, a child whose memories would not be able to form in time to remember her. There was denial.

When he is older, you will have that conversation with him. *Is there anything you remember of her? Any texture? Any sound? Smell?* You were a little older than your son's age when your mother lost her father. Too young to really know him. So it goes. People as fundamental as the sky, gone before they can be shared by future generations. You remember a little, your grandfather's arms, the faded Navy tattoos, shreds of tobacco on the table top and the little machine he used to roll cigarettes, him carefully stirring a pan of cocoa. And that is all. From so little, can a person be summoned? You remember London, where he lived with your Nan. London one winter in the Seventies while you were visiting, under all that snow, a buried city, alleys of ice, cars gone missing, frozen taps. Ever since, London has seemed in your imagination a broken winter city. You have conflated these memories, of course. Your consciousness wasn't formed, you were just a receptacle. You have often wondered about memories that are not your own, memories of what you've been told, implanted, hereditary, even genetic. Your grandfather was a boy soldier at the Somme, one of so few who survived. He spent four decades at sea. *HOLD FAST* was inked on his knuckles. In your mind, it's easy to see those words, faded, bled through the skin. Yellow gas. Drenched wool. Wounds in his legs that would swallow the shrapnel and keep it as a heavy souvenir. Those green, incalculable waves, south of the equator. But, then, you've read all this, seen films, heard family stories. Your cells, your neurons, your imagination have all been manipulated.

As your son sleeps, you whisper things about your mother and your mother's history to him. *She loved butter. She always sneezed three times. Her perfume rose a few notes above her skin. She hid much of her identity. Her grandparents crossed the border in a farm wagon to get out of their country. The rest, the unnumbered, were never spoken about. The great stirred cauldron of Europe, where so many were and are repelled, sent in to exile, east and west, again and again.* This too feels occult. What order of gifts are you trying to give him? But, here, now, in the calm warmth of the car, holding the child, a hurricane surrounding the county and shutting everything down, you are dimensional in ways you can't comprehend. You can feel the river of what has passed and what is coming. The morning sky is dark. Birds are being blown between branches, forming shapes, auguring. There are selves within your self. The ones behind are unreachable, unstructured, like skins that have been shed. The ones in front – you can't know how far they extend. They can only watch, only witness your aloneness, your struggles. They can't promise you any happiness, and if they could, you would not believe it. This rain is not helping: savage, unrelenting, strange even for here, making it hard to see anything clearly or think clearly. The rain incants, has its voice, its rhythm, it is the method used to reach another state, it allows you to enter, if you wish to. What you sense is mutability. The terror of being taken, ahead, into sheer darkness. What is coming? Not just this lesson of a dying mother. But travel into – you can do no more than intuit. You suspect your dreams are communicating far more destruction than you have interpreted, and in this you are correct. The future is a window, which cannot be opened until it is opened.

Your mother's coffin is white. Lightweight. It is made of wool, from this district of wool. It is waiting quietly for her at the undertaker's. It will be covered with the flowers she loved most. Six of you will bear it from the car into the church, then to the cemetery – you and your closest cousin at the front, your tall, quiet, fourteen-year-old nephew at the back, your brother, father, and one other, who is already turning away, and will remain faceless. Your cousin has farmed sheep for years, hefting animals onto her shoulders, bringing them into the sheds in winter gales, for lambing, or in sickness. It is one of the hardest occupations. Though she worries she is not capable, you know she is. You are worrying too, about this duty. Are you strong enough? Will you remain upright, sure-footed? Will you break down under grief? And, yes, who, after this is done, as it must be done, tomorrow, or the next day, whenever the rain permits, who will carry you?

This, you can't be told. Stories are the currency of past lives. Families, lovers, enemies, friends. You do not understand yet, who you will lose, who you will become, who will arrive. We are, all of us, sudden travellers in the world, blind, passing each other, reaching out hands, missing, sometimes taking hold. But, sooner than you think, after this flood, after the darkness, the loss,

the loneliness, someone is going to take your hand
and tell a story about the death of his grandfather.
It is a story about displacement, about expulsion
from a homeland, again, always, thousands fleeing
for the border, left un-belonging, making a new
home. It is a story about snow as well, snow in the
suburbs of a city you have not yet seen, but will
see, vast, continental, the city of all cities, where, in
the year of the grandfather's death, water flooded
the basement walls and froze to ice, the ground
was so hard, so locked, the family worried no
grave could be dug, though dug it was. The men
carried the coffin, from home to mosque,
traditional pall bearers where no such occupation
exists, rotating positions, bringing in new arms
every so often to renew their strength. He carried
it too, this teller, this future traveller. The story will
feel so familiar to you. You will begin to understand
that those who suffer, suffer the same. In this
condition, we are never alone. And in love, there
are no divides. The heaviness that you are going to
feel, when that white box is upon your shoulder,
and even after it is set down, lowered, buried, and
for years to follow, will, for the first time, become
less. But not yet.

First, these floods, the waterlogged cemetery,
people toiling to get this ruined English patch
clear and open and ready to receive. Bags of muck

and silt dumped at the gates. Promissory clouds in the west. The undertakers will be arriving in a while to assess the situation, to see whether the small yellow digger will be able to get in and do its work. He is young, the head of the funeral home – forty perhaps, Irish, un-phased by rain's catastrophe, by any catastrophe. You have fallen, after only a day or two in his company, in love with him, and will love him for the duration of this event. His immaculate suit. Hands, with the high veins of one used to ferrying awkward human loads. He purveys the calm and rightness of what must happen at life's end. Astonishing, you think, the care with which a stranger might be tended by strangers. *Don't panic,* he says, *just don't panic.* This is his standard catchphrase, panic being, you realise, one of death's main ingredients. *Ring me,* he says, *day or night, if you want to come and see her. She is your mother. She is yours.* Your father has visited several times, kept her body company, given her the recent news, brought her a letter from you with cuttings of hair from you and your son, brought her some sloe gin, it's brewing season. She is still his wife.

But she is no longer your mother. Atoms, dreams, gods, whatever the new state, she is gone. That is what you wanted to see in the mortuary. You wanted to see that she had been taken, that she was vacant. And she was, like a bad photograph of herself that failed to capture any soul, or any real likeness. Her body, which was your shared pre-language, which is the language your son speaks with you now, was empty, altered, altering, chemicals notwithstanding. Matter can't last its separation from energy. To say you could not touch her isn't true. You touched her hair, very gently, a coward, knowing this would be the least cold part, while your brother's wife did the rest. And that was the last time you saw her. That was when you gave her up.

The baby stirs, constructs a new nested position under your arm. If he were to open his eyes you could compare their colour to hers, which is very similar. Even now you know that will be a consolation over the coming years. You will say it readily to people. *They have the same blue... like denim.* It has occurred to you that you have been neither a very good mother nor a very good daughter over the last year. Caught between two extreme experiences, incoming and outgoing, to put it bluntly, there was some kind of internal paralysis, which has led to double failure. People have been kind, mostly. *It's an impossible situation,* they've said, *all you can do is cope, look after your child, tell your mother you love her.* Of course, there are expectations, unspoken, and judgements. You are a woman, after all. But you have fed and dressed and cleaned the baby. You have arranged his immunisations, taken him to the swimming pool, read and sung to him. You've kept up with the antenatal group – there's a lot of tea and cake involved, chat about managerial blow jobs, wilted breasts for the ones who are no longer nursing, even talk of second babies, *may as well get it all over and done with*... You have called and visited your mother, helped her up the stairs and into the car for appointments, told her the wig looks great – *really natural* – and in fact it did, mashed her food, helped her to the commode, cleaned up, done as much as you could. Though it is your father who has quite superbly and unfalteringly and sometimes impatiently cared for her, every day. You have operated in the capacities you've had to. But you can't say that you felt truly present, or receptive, or mindful. Where were you? There, but not there. Waiting for something to change.

Now, you must wait out the rain, see what the earth will allow. Ceremonies can happen anytime, words, the songs of grief, celebrations – these things are fine and lost like smoke. It is the last deep ritual of commitment that humans battle to make. The relinquishment. Practical surrender. Fire or soil or salt. The sea. You can see the stress on your father's and brother's faces. They know the importance of this last destination. They know they are fighting, not just with elements, the earth, the bloody ridiculous weather, but with their own mortal machinery. Their voices are becoming more and more anxious. *When is it going to give up? Pass me that shovel. Do you think the water's going down in the corner?* Your brother tries to check the weather app on his phone, but, surrounded by hills and clouds, there is no signal. As a hundred years ago, the sky is the only way to predict. And in the west – more anvil clouds, thick, forge of the storm. Your brother is squatting by the drain; his elbows are dripping. Your father stands looking at the trickling slope, on which is her plot, and his too, when it's time. His head is bent. He might be weeping. He might be praying or thinking nothing. In this graveyard lie the bones of his own father, who died long ago, whom you never knew at all. You could place the baby on the seat of the car, and go to them. But you don't.

Wait. That is all you have to do. It is a lesson from your childhood in this place. Nothing is unchanging. Rain that seems unstoppable, that seems impossible to see through, that keeps coming down, obscuring the world, washing away time, will end. Like everything else, it is only passing spirit.

And then, you know how it will be, you don't need to be told, just imagine a version. Breaking cloud, sky with discernible colour, fantastic-seeming sunlight. The rain will lift. The river will recede. Your father and brother will have dragged enough branches and mess clear of the drains for the flood to disperse. The little yellow digger will chug down the road, bow wave before it, churned wake following, and it will toil over the uneven ground to the place your father is standing now. It will set its bucket down, ready to bring up mud and roots and slop. The grave-digger, a man in his Seventies who calls himself just 'Fosser', like his previous Roman cousins, like some kind of preternatural ancient, will do something he has not done for years, possibly since he was an apprentice: he will build temporary wooden struts to keep the sodden walls of the grave from falling. And, listen, if you really need a sign, now, that something better is coming, that you will survive, that you will one day travel through kinder times, here it is. When Fosser arrives, he will climb out of the cab and will stand looking out at the valley's expanse of water for a moment, and he will come over to the car and knock on the window, which you will put down, and he will say one word to you: *Bosphorus*. Later, you will remember this. You will remember it while standing on board a ship, holding the rusted rail, rain hammering the surface of the Strait, domes and minarets and towers rising out of the mist, calls of gulls, and a man's face turned towards you, his heat against your chest as you make the crossing, not really from west to east, or east to west, but from suffering to happiness. Coincidence? Fate? Just Fosser, mentioning his last holiday, perhaps. These labourers of the other realms, of portals, these keepers of the beyond – can they predict, can they see what you cannot?

Tomorrow. Tomorrow, the hearse will swim through the remaining tides and lumber gracefully up the unmade lane to the house, looking like a black swan. Freesias will line its polished wooden shelf. Inside, the white wool coffin you have, as a family, chosen, will cosset your mother. You will put on a long black coat and red gloves, boots. Your oldest school friend will come and mind the baby – the first day of him being fully weaned, though you had not planned it this way. The church will only be half full – not because your mother wasn't loved, but because the roads and railways right up the western half of the country are shut. Chaos for the mourners, chaos for commuters, for everyone, homes abandoned, bridges washed away, power out. You will stand up and speak at the service, as will your father and brother, you will all manage to get through it, and your niece, only twelve years old, for God's sake, will read a poem about hearts within hearts, flawlessly, and she will seem so much older. Your shoulder, the shoulder upon which you usually set the baby after feeding, the shoulder where the strap of your bag hangs every day, and where there will be, in a year or two, as a protective talisman, or instructions for living, a small blue tattoo with the words *Vive ut Vivas,* your shoulder will bear one sixth of the weight of the coffin, of the reduced, insubstantial body of your mother. The churchgoers will process through the village behind the hearse, as is tradition here, to the cemetery, where the gates will be open, where the undertakers will steward you across difficult slippery ground, like outriders, your boots will gather mud up the heels, but you will not stumble, you will carry her, you will carry her, all the way, you will carry her, steadily, so will your cousin, and the four other bearers, with an unrelieved ache, and someone will have remembered roses to let go into the grave, and the gorse on the moorland, still flowering wildly, will smell almost like jasmine, and the rain will hold off, and the mountains will neither pity nor forgive you.

Van Rensburg's Card

Kiare Ladner

GRETA DROVE FAST ALONG the rural road leading away from the small school where she taught maths. Fields of sugarcane mangy with drought gave way to mottled hills and grasslands. She sped past a scattered settlement of rondawels, some the colour of mud, others pale blue or green. Then a dry river bed, a couple of crudely penned kraals of nguni cattle and a rusted orange minivan in a ditch. She was bound to get another ticket to add to the mounting stack in the Ukhamba basket but she kept her foot on the pedal and turned the air con up.

Eighteen months ago, she used to take pleasure in the drive between teaching and home. She would open the windows wide and blast out Miriam Makeba or Ella Fitzgerald or the Inuit throat-singing CD her daughter had sent from Canada. Tapping on the steering wheel, she'd sing and bop to the beat like an old fool imitation of her students, Fikile or Buhle. But these days music, any kind of music, was too much. The speedometer climbed from 120 to 130. Children, perhaps those she taught, or their brothers or sisters, had been throwing stones at cars here recently. Going fast didn't lessen the risk of being hit but it did help get the stretch over with.

What she dreaded wasn't having the windscreen shattered, or even being a sitting duck for further violence, so much as the hassle of having to stop and talk to people. All morning she'd looked forward to being alone. Not in her home in Fairview Gardens complex with its quarry tiles and wildflower bedspreads and navy and cream batik curtains with ties – but out and about in the bustling distraction of the mall; out and about having a meal. She shifted her fleshy buttocks against the beaded seat-cover picturing The Fayre and Square's lunchtime buffet. A plate piled high with mealie bread, butternut and feta salad, chargrilled, smoky aubergine and cold, spicy frikkadels.

Until recently she'd never gone for a meal on her own anywhere; not a proper one, not a lunch or a dinner. Years back in Gauteng, she'd imagined herself doing it. Calling in sick to the boys' school where she taught and driving to a hotel in the centre of Jo'burg for a steak with monkey gland sauce. Or catching a minibus to Chinatown for sticky jasmine rice and sweet and sour prawns. But before Harold died, eating out was something they did only together. She'd always told him exactly where she was and what she was doing as if he were her keeper.

Quite possibly, he'd thought it was the other way around.

*

At an island plumed with cycads and palms, Greta turned onto the dual carriageway leading to the city and the sea rather than the single-lane carriageway that led inland and home. When Nikki was little, the highway had been bordered by subtropical grasslands that were undeveloped almost all the way to the coast. They used to come here for the Easter holidays and this last part of the drive was one of excited anticipation. 'Can you taste the salt on your lips? Who can see the sea? Twenty cents for the one who sees it first!'

After the mall sprang up, they'd stop for a few essentials: food and dish liquid and insect spray and plenty of bleach. Nikki's disappointment at the delay would be appeased by a bag of candyfloss from the machine in the supermarket. Later, while

Greta unpacked and cleaned the rented cottage to their kind of spic-and-span, Harold would take Nikki for a walk on the beach. 'Just a walk,' Harold would say. 'We'll leave swimming for tomorrow.' But they'd come back with the hems of their clothes dripping. 'A big wave, Mummy! It knocked right into us!'

The drive, the place, seemed to Greta not to be this drive, this place. The country had changed but it wasn't that; the memory itself seemed to belong in a parallel universe. Which was just the kind of whimsical thing Harold would've said. He'd have said it and she'd have been irritated with him for saying it. Now she was frustrated at not being able to be irritated. She pressed her thickened index nail into the cushion of her thumb.

Most people heading off the highway towards the mall took the main road to the multi-storey parkade; but Greta preferred the side road that curved around the back. She liked to park in the open air under a giant-leaved fig tree closest to her favourite wing. She thought of it as the Spanish wing, not because of the new Spanish restaurant, El Cerdito (a glitzy place where people sat on high stools and ate from ridiculously minute plates), but because of the relaxed, sunny, rustic feel of the rest of the wing that she associated with Spain as she imagined it.

Today, as she neared the turnoff, a sign announced in beaded lights: '*ROAD CLOSED FOR CONSTRUCTION.*' Aside from a bulldozer with its blade in the air, there didn't seem to be much construction underway, so Greta kept indicating as if the sign might change; as if, in capitulation to her refusal to accept it, its lights might bead differently to say something else. She was just veering towards the outside of her lane when a man in a high-vis jacket leapt into the middle of the road, gesticulating angrily, furiously, at her to get back.

When she resumed her place in the queue crawling towards the main entrance of the parkade, the white SUV behind her gave a needlessly prolonged hoot. The driver had a helmet of mahogany hair, huge bug-eyed sunglasses and a carload of kids. She flashed her hand at Greta as if to say that she was crazy. With the fairies! Cuckoo! She kept flashing all the way to the ticket barrier. 'Oh, cuckoo, cuckoo to you too,' Greta muttered and flashed her hand back.

Only as she went under the boom did she realise: the woman had been trying to show that her indicator was on. She supposed she'd left it on since the turnoff, or even further back, the dual carriageway. Grudgingly, she steered in the direction she was indicating, going down where she least wanted to go, into the basement of the parkade.

Before learning to drive, Greta had had nightmares about losing control on a parkade ramp. Though in over fifty years of driving it hadn't happened, the fear hadn't disappeared. If anything, it was worse now that there was a real possibility that her arms would go numb and then her legs. That one day her body would simply conk out like Harold's had. He was lucky he'd been at home with her there to look after him. But only one of them could have that pass. Now it was all used up, thanks Harold. Now, there was nothing to do but accept being mortified in public before actual rigor mortis set in.

Not yet though. Having made it down the ramp, Greta exited uneventfully at level minus one. She found a parking space to get into without needing to reverse, and switched the car off. Then she heaved herself from the seat using the door frame for leverage. It was a recent development, this struggle to get up. It was only from low seats, and it wasn't age, it was the extra weight. Reversible, she'd definitely reverse it before Nikki next came over. Relieved there was nobody about to see her, she smoothed her sack-like dress across the indents the seat-cover beads had left on her buttocks and legs. She locked the car, put her keys in her large, navy handbag and strode to the lift.

The air in the basement was hot, smelly and stale. She wondered if there was any chance that Nikki would come over this year; she'd made no mention of it in their calls but that didn't mean no necessarily. Greta pressed the luminous pink arrow and waited. She felt a bit shaky, a bit nauseous. Eating too much these days didn't make her less hungry: the sugar highs caused sugar dips; her blood sugar levels were all over the place. Impatient, she decided to take the stairs instead. Halfway up she regretted it; as well as the stink of urine, there were broad, shiny puddles. The fluorescent lighting flickered and a horrid fluttering or scurrying seemed to follow her. One moment she thought that it came from a corner at her feet, the next that it was just above her head. 'Scoot!' she said loudly as she stomped her health shoes up the last few steps. 'Scoot, scoot!' as she exited the stairwell into the mall.

An Indian man, slight as a sprig of dill, turned to stare at her. He started to say or ask her something but she hurried on her way. She was disorientated; she didn't usually come into the mall through this entrance. She stopped only when she reached four mirrored columns that stood like sentries at an unfamiliar intersection of shops. Breathless and clammy with sweat, she splayed her hand in the air. Was the air con working?

In the column opposite her, she saw a stranger flapping about in a flowery brown smock. A Seventies preggy dress was what it was actually, back from when she'd been expecting with Nikki. She'd found it in the kist a few weeks ago and thought, that'll be useful now that you're a fat old hag.

A fat old hag.

She reached into her handbag. Behind her book and a stiff, handmade card, she found a pack of pocket tissues. She blotted the perspiration from her forehead, her nose, her upper lip, then used the card to fan herself.

Since Harold's death, she often caught herself imagining she and Nikki going for meals together. Eating grilled seafood at the Wild Coast Sun, sharing a lamb potjie in the Midlands, sipping green smoothies in the nearby nursery cafe. It was impossible, of course; Nikki lived thousands of miles away, on another continent, in another hemisphere. And Greta hadn't expected her to come back, though it was what some of the younger generation did these days. She hadn't even expected Nikki to come over more often, for month-long holidays with Jayne and little

Denzel, like Elma's son and his family did.

A trickle of perspiration ran down Greta's upper arm to her elbow and plopped like a tear onto the floor.

She stopped fanning. She knew where she was now. Beyond the mirrored columns was the smart black and white signage for Woollies. The trolleys and the buckets of flowers, the cheerful bunches of roses and proteas and chrysanthemums. Further along, she'd come upon the homely neighbourhood of restaurants that blended together with their yellows and reds and wooden tables and chairs and ornamental kegs and hanging garlic and onions and copper pots and pans: the Spanish wing.

*

Although Greta liked the idea of choosing a restaurant on a whim, the place she ended up was usually the first she'd had in mind. So despite lingering outside Ocean Queen to read the specials on the board, despite being drawn to the waft of garlic and olives as she passed Antonio's Italian, the restaurant she went into was The Fayre and Square.

The table she wanted had a view of the square with the fountains but also of the buffet.

She was mid-stride towards it when cool fingers stopped her. 'Excuse me, ma'am?' A woman in a silky oyster pantsuit with a soft, powdery scent lightly manoeuvred her back to a sign propped up like sheet music on a stand: *'PLEASE WAIT HERE TO BE SEATED.'*

Greta stood meekly where she'd been put. She gazed across the half-empty restaurant. The table she'd coveted had been a particularly good one because from there she'd be able to see the food before going over to serve herself up. She'd avoid looking foolishly indecisive or ending up with some random hotchpotch on her plate.

'Afternoon, ma'am.' A waitress in smart black trousers with a black apron tied neatly around her waist stepped forward. 'I'm Lindiwe. Can I take you through?' Greta focused on the name badge pinned to Lindiwe's white shirt pocket while steeling herself to make her request – but Lindiwe gestured towards the table of her own accord. 'That one, over there?'

After placing a napkin on Greta's lap, Lindiwe set three menus in front of her: the wine list, the specials, and the à la carte.

'Would you like something to drink, ma'am? A glass of sauvignon blanc? Or a shiraz?'

Greta wasn't much of a drinker, least of all on her own. But not wanting to answer Lindiwe's kindness with rejection, she said, 'A glass of shiraz would be fine, thanks.'

While Lindiwe went off to fetch the wine, Greta arranged her spectacles, her phone and her book in front of her. The props made being alone more acceptable. Ever since an elderly couple had sent a grandchild to ask her to join their table, she'd made sure to have her excuses to hand.

'Here's your shiraz, ma'am.' Lindiwe put a glass as big as a vase in front of Greta.

'Oh... goodness.'

'Can I tell you about the specials?'

Greta shook her head. 'You know what, Lindiwe? I'm going to go for the buffet.'

'Certainly, ma'am. My colleague will bring a plate.'

Greta sipped her wine and waited. She couldn't see the frikkadels from where she sat but she could see thick slices of silver-pink corned beef. She used to make a good corned beef hash but that was before her cooking went indigenous. She couldn't remember why in hell she'd battened onto that idea; Harold had loved her corned beef hash. She sipped some more wine and forced her focus back to the table. The butternut and feta salad was in a large cut glass bowl, and although there weren't chargrilled aubergines there was chargrilled something else, tomatoes or peppers.

The mealie bread was almost finished, but the last hunk was a generous one, thick and crusty from the pan. A couple of policemen working their way around the table stopped in front of it. Greta tilted her wine back and found she'd finished it.

At the far end of the buffet, a stack of dinner plates waited on a copper heating device. Looking around to see if anybody was bringing one over to her, Greta inadvertently caught Lindiwe's eye. 'Another glass of the shiraz, ma'am?'

'Actually, I wanted to ask about my plate –'

'Certainly, ma'am. My colleague will bring it over.'

'Okay, thanks.'

Greta opened her book. It was Nadine Gordimer's last: *No Time Like the Present*. She stared at the thick fuzz of words covering the page. Then from her bag she took the envelope she'd used to fan herself.

'Excuse me, ma'am?' Lindiwe was back – with a refill of the shiraz. She beamed as she put it down.

Greta couldn't summon the energy to correct the misunderstanding. 'Thank you, Lindiwe,' she said.

While gazing over the wine at the fountains, Greta carefully removed the card from the envelope. Fountains in a drought. How much water did they lose each day to evaporation? How much did that amount to in a month, a year? It was the kind of question she could set her students. She let the wine trickle down her throat. The front of the card was illustrated with a charcoal sketch of flowers. A nip of impasto-yellow paint lighted the petal of one of them. When her students got stuck trying to solve a tricky maths problem, she told them: 'Sometimes the way with these things is to leave them and come back, sometimes when you come back to them they fall into place, make sense.'

The card had been slipped under her door a week after Harold's death. She'd ignored the bell but through the window she'd seen Arthur van Rensburg tramping down the hill. He was elderly, a few years older than her, but spritely, that silly word, was how everyone referred to him. He lived at the far end of the complex; at the bottom, near the creek. The residents complained about the presence of rats down there but she couldn't imagine him being fazed by rats. He had large, protruding ears and ginger-grey hair, a bit long, a bit scraggly. Although there was an old mustard Datsun in his carport, he went everywhere by bicycle with a soft leather rucksack on his back.

He might have made the card himself. It didn't take much of a stretch to picture him making a card like that. Greta opened it and put her glasses on although she knew the words by heart.

I have heard of your loss. I lost my own wife ten years ago this Christmas. The emptiness was hard to bear.
I still miss her every day although I have become closer to my children and grandchildren in the interrum.

She slowed down; she concentrated.

I have found it helpful to view death as a part of what shapes and re-shapes a family. Not solely as the end but as a link to new visions of being together. Pushing the way forward as the family grows and thrives.
Arthur

Greta took her glasses off .

PS If you'd like a cup of tea with one of my survival biscuits (made from a tried and trusted old recipe!) do come over. It's No. 37.

She folded her glasses and put them back in their case.

When she'd first read Van Rensburg's card she'd been offended. Death as *a link to new visions of being together* – what kind of rubbish was that? What did he know of her life? Of her family, who was only one child, who didn't even live here?

And *as the family grows and thrives*. How presumptuous.

After chucking the card in the kitchen bin, she'd sat for a long time gazing out, away from the complex, over the hills that were still overgrown with eucalyptus trees and wild bamboo, the home to vast troupes of vervet monkeys. The big life events seemed to make people you hardly knew feel they had the right to intrude. She'd thought of when she was pregnant with Nikki, how she'd hated everyone touching her, patting her belly, offering advice. Admittedly she and Harold had become fairly isolated in their retirement, so this had been a less participatory event than that, but still. She watched the sun turn as red as a clot, then drop down behind the dusty hills. She'd been throwing all the cards she received in the bin. She didn't want them around, found absolutely no comfort in them. But this one, she felt, Van Rensburg's, deserved a worse fate.

Wiping bits of eggshell from the envelope, she'd imagined Nikki saying, 'Ignore it, Mom, he's just a well meaning fool.' Was he, though, just a fool? She recalled a residents' meeting where he'd made a clever suggestion about the drainage, offering to come up with some plans for free. Had he been a civil engineer then? She didn't think so; rather… a one-time activist, an anthropologist, was that it? The civil engineer might have been a member of his growing, thriving family. Yet if he was an intelligent man, a good man, then it was worse, this insensitivity. Then she had a right to show him that he'd hurt her, that he'd caused harm. And so, after much reflection, she'd decided to return the card. Opened, the envelope torn at the top, obviously read, obviously rejected. She wondered if he would be upset by that. She thought of him flying on his bike down the road that led from the complex into the town. She thought of that scent he had about him, not dirty but a leathery, coffee scent.

She'd intended to walk down to No. 37 as soon as the streetlights came on. But instead, by the glow that burned through her living room window, she'd ended up reading the card again. It was something she did sometimes with emails from Nikki. Sometimes what Nikki had written would go rotten in her head, would seem weighed down with implied accusations – but later, on re-reading it, she'd find the intimations were her own; Nikki's words were innocent, completely innocent.

On the second reading of Arthur van Rensburg's card Greta had been similarly less convinced of her right to be offended. His message was different to the others she'd received but possibly no worse. It was free of the expected clichés. It didn't say 'sorry'. Or that horrible distancing 'sorry for your loss'. Or worst of all, 'I can't imagine how it feels...' Well bloody make the effort to imagine then, she wanted to retort. No, Arthur's card was at least an honest attempt to communicate. Even the cup of tea was more real, more specific than the ubiquitous, 'if there's anything we can do'.

By the light of her bedside lamp, giving the card a third reading and a fourth, Greta's feelings had wavered again. Was the message smug, clumsy and presumptuous? Or cryptic but profound? In the weeks and months that followed, because she couldn't make up her mind, because she had the kind of mind that fiddled with puzzles endlessly, that struggled to leave what was irresolvable alone – but also because the card was the most consolation anyone had offered her, because really she had no consolations at all – she hadn't returned the card. She'd hung onto it.

And now, as she finished off her second glass of wine in The Fayre and Square, another perspective suggested itself. What if Arthur van Rensburg knew more or was at least more perceptive than she realised? What if, instead of assuming that she had a close thriving family, he had been trying to tell her that it could change?

That she could change it? Anthropology was the study of human behaviour, after all, wasn't it?

Sunlight caught the fountain, sparkling on the water, making it almost too bright to look at.

shapes and re-shapes.

As it was, Nikki initiated all the contact in their relationship. A phone call every second Saturday night, an email every fortnight in between. It hurt, the rigidity, the sense of duty this implied. When Nikki had been in her twenties, her psychologist had suggested she determine the boundaries of their relationship. New, healthy boundaries might lead to a new, healthy parent-daughter relationship, Dr Oosthuizen had said. Quite likely she'd been right at the time, but twenty years on hadn't the usefulness of the attitude expired?

The restaurant shifted like a stage set in a breeze as Greta stood up. Should she be the one to make a call, to take the initiative for once? What would the time be now in Montreal? Lunchtime here made it early morning there. In a couple of hours Nikki would be at work. If only Harold could know that she was no longer a security guard but an account manager – now, there in itself was an example of *re-shaping*; a change that Nikki had made, a *pushing forward* she had done on her own.

Greta strode over to the buffet. The last hunk of mealie bread had still not been taken. She helped herself to a plate from the pile on the copper stand. If the call led to further developments she'd need to make some changes herself. Tomorrow. Tomorrow she'd start watching her weight. She'd eat small, balanced meals and go for powerwalks. This lunch would be her final indulgence; she might as well make the most of it. Even with her privileged view of the spread, she hadn't seen that there were chafing dishes of hot foods too. Roast lamb and chicken and potatoes and gravy and chops and rice and ribs. She helped herself to everything.

Back at her table, Greta abandoned herself to the soothing mindlessness of eating. She alternated between the meats and the salads and the veg in a sort of trance. All of it was wonderfully flavoursome and her gluttonous feast had almost been reduced to a regular-sized plateful when Lindiwe appeared.

She looked terribly flustered. 'Sorry, ma'am. You're supposed to weigh what you take first –'

The drumstick Greta was gnawing at cracked. 'Pardon?'

'You're supposed to weigh the plate. After you've served yourself, you weigh it. Then we know what to charge you.'

Greta tried to take the bone out of her mouth discretely.

'There are the scales, ma'am.' Lindiwe pointed towards a silver surface by the till. 'You weigh your food and then we give you a slip.'

'Well, that's new!'

'No ma'am. It's been like this for four months.'

Four months? Greta pushed her offending plate back and some gravy sloshed onto the table. 'I don't quite know what to do then. I suppose you could weigh what's left and – double it?'

Lindiwe sucked in her lips. 'Don't worry, ma'am. I'll just weigh what's left.'

'No, no. I insist on paying for what I had –'

'It'll be fine, ma'am. If I can just take your plate.'

Gravy dripped from the plate as Lindiwe lifted it. Greta still had the splintered drumstick in her hand. She hesitated, then added it to the other bones to be weighed, a chop, a marrow bone and a wing.

When Lindiwe returned, she wiped the surface where the gravy had spilled. The cloth left an arc of small dots and a strong reek of damp. She tucked the ticket under the plate. 'Another glass of the shiraz, ma'am?'

Greta flapped her hand dismissively at Lindiwe. It was a hurtful gesture someone had made to her once. A man from the complex she'd bumped into at the nursery, after she'd gotten carried away talking about strelitzias. Go, go, you are a nuisance, it said.

Since the gesture churned up a sick feeling in Greta still, when Lindiwe simply interpretted it as a signal for yet another glass of wine, Greta was too stunned to send the glass back. Instead, when Lindiwe had gone, she leaned over to the potted plant behind the table. Aglaonemas were known for their hardiness. About to dump her wine among its two-tone leaves, she sensed somebody watching her.

The bug-eyed sunglasses woman from the SUV was standing at the buffet table with a toddler on her hip.

Greta withdrew from the Aglaonema and put the glass to her lips. She gulped at the wine as if it were a medication she had to have and forced her food down to soak it up. She crammed heaped forkfuls into her mouth, less aware now of taste than of texture, the dense difficult textures that required effort to be chewed into pulp. Hard bits of grain, husks, gristle that caught in her teeth, even the mealie bread that she'd been keeping specially became a chewy wodge to be got through. The whole process was no longer pleasurable, but mechanical. Shove, cram, chew, swallow. Repeat, repeat.

★

No sooner had Greta paid for her meal than she began to feel nauseous. She hurried through the Spanish wing and followed a restroom sign up an escalator to a fast food court. She rushed past KFC and Wimpy and Nandos and Steers through two sets of doors into a cubicle where she threw up. Never again would she visit The Fayre and Square, that was for sure! She flushed the toilet and with it the whole darned experience away.

In the corridor, drying off her fingers on a tissue from her bag, she almost walked past the empty lift. On a different floor, it wasn't where she'd expected it to be. As the doors closed behind her, she pressed the button with a '1' on it. Nothing happened. She looked for a button to re-open the doors but couldn't see any, so she pressed the '1' again. She held her thumb down hard. The light underneath the '1' flickered but the lift didn't move. All six sides of the lift were the same; a dull, blurrily reflective metal. She looked at the brown blurry distortions of herself.

Prince, the pop star whose posters Nikki had had on her walls as a teenager, had died alone in a lift recently. That was pretty much all Greta knew about him but she'd cried when she read it. It was such a shoddy end for anybody. To give up, to let go, in such circumstances. Harold had given up and let go too. They'd been arguing, and he'd asked her why she was with him, and she'd said, 'Who said love is pity?' She gave the lift's '1' button an almighty punch. Why the hell had she said that? What the hell kind of person said such a thing?

A dark streak of blood smeared the control panel. Greta flexed her hand a couple of times: old skin was dramatic; it bled profusely. She felt about in her bag for a tissue to wipe the panel with but her pack was empty. She found Harold's hanky but she couldn't bring herself to use it on the lift. He'd kept his hankies immaculate, white and ironed and folded in neat squares; they were for his skin, or hers when he lent them.

She stood staring at the panel while blood dripped from her knuckles. Then she realised: '1' was the floor she was on. The lift hadn't moved because she'd been targeting the wrong button. With her index finger, she lightly tapped '-1', and at once the lift descended.

*

Greta held her bloody hand, wrapped up in Harold's hanky, against her breast and felt as if it was another creature that she held. As if the beating of her heart that she felt there was rather another creature's heart.

When she got to her car she took the hanky off. The bleeding had stopped. Her legs felt heavy, her whole body felt heavy, although her head felt light. Light and breezy and streaming with sunshine. She thought of putting on some music, Mozart or Chopin, she was in the mood to play something… but she also didn't want to taint this feeling she had in any way, with any other influence.

shape and reshape. shape and reshape.

She wanted desperately to phone Nikki with this lightness and − compassion, that was it, compassion was what she felt. She'd say, oh it would be something to do with how she understood, now, how Nikki'd felt when she'd self-harmed. The secret was not to overthink the conversation too much, not to commit herself to the precise words. It would be better if it happened naturally. The words would come once they were talking; she'd find them, she'd improvise.

After the call she'd go down to Arthur van Rensburg's. No. 37. Yes. They'd sit on his stoep, eating his survival cookies and she'd tell him just a bit of what had happened. And when he offered to walk her home, back to her place at the top of the complex, she'd say, 'Oh no, it's fine, Arthur, I have my car here. Always best to be independent.' And he'd say, 'Well it was great having you over, do come again.' And she'd say, 'Thank you, Arthur, I will.' And then, when she got back to her place there'd be an email in her inbox from Nikki saying that she wanted to continue with their phone conversation in person. That it had been so good to chat.

Hush, Greta. She was letting herself get too carried away. Best to phone Nikki first, then take it from there. Yet, the more she thought about it, the more she thought she didn't want to phone Nikki from home. She wanted to have this conversation somewhere they'd never spoken before. Somewhere peaceful. Natural. Untarnished.

A few kilometres before Fairview Garden complex, she took a turnoff onto a dirt road that went up a hill. She'd often wondered about this road but had never driven along it. It was a private road that probably belonged to a private game farm though there was no farmhouse in sight. At the top of the hill she pulled over by a cluster of acacias and switched the car off.

She turned the key so that the air conditioning went off too. A small herd of impala scattered down the slope, into the bushwillow, into the veld. The air was hot and dry and dusty; she cleared her throat and took out her cell. She scrolled past

Doctor, Dentist, Garage, Insurance. Before she could change her mind she swiped Nikki's number.

*

Nikki's phone rang and rang. Then, 'Hi, please leave a message and I'll get back to you.' Greta tried to think of a message to leave but none came to her. She ended the call. Then she thought, now Nikki would have to listen to a blank message. It would be irritating, or worse, seem manipulative, forcing Nikki to phone her back. She didn't want to start their *re-shaping* on such a wrong footing, so she swiped Nikki's number again.

When the phone stopped ringing the second time, she waited, ready to speak, but the voicemail didn't click into place. She heard some background noises, a few people laughing. Then Nikki's voice, uncharacteristically small and hesitant, 'Hello?'

'Nikki, hi!'

'Mom, are you all right?'

'Yes. Everything's fine.'

'I got a fright.'

'Sorry, I didn't intend to give you a fright.' Greta stopped herself. She was sounding annoyed. That was the last thing she wanted. 'Are you busy, then?'

'I'm at work.'

Work, Greta thought. Work where she'd been for forty years, interrupted for any slightest need of Nikki's. Called to the phone in the secretary's office. Mom, I forgot my lunch. Mom, I forgot my swimming costume. 'I thought you started later.'

'It's already ten, Mom,' Nikki said. 'But I can talk.'

'Have you changed to summertime, then?'

'Yes, the clocks moved back last weekend.'

'You remember Elma from the complex?' Greta said. 'Her son, Victor, missed a flight once because he hadn't realised the clocks had changed. He says they don't advertise it there at all. Everyone is just meant to understand without anybody saying anything –'

'It's okay that you forgot, Mom.'

Greta swallowed her irritation. She knew she ought to swallow what she was about to say next too. 'Luckily the flight he missed was an internal one. He said it wasn't a mistake he'd make again. Maybe it was for the best, given all the flights he makes to South Africa with his family these days. They fly out two, three times a year –'

'They must have a lot of money to afford that,' Nikki said.

'I don't think so. He's a junior researcher.'

'Maybe his wife makes the money.'

'I don't know. But they don't do things extravagantly, Nikki. Last time, they all went up the coast together and stayed in huts. Elma said it was dirt cheap. She said she'd give me the information if I wanted. The only thing is, it's best to book in advance. Especially if it's around a holiday like Christmas...'

Greta held her breath. She'd said too much. It never used to happen when Harold was around but now sometimes she couldn't hold back. Still, maybe this was *pushing forward*? The colours of the surrounding hills appeared heightened in the late afternoon light. The greens and yellows and golds and browns, fading to blues as they grew more distant.

'Jayne bought Denzel his first snowboard the other day,' said Nikki. 'It was on sale.'

'That's nice,' said Greta.

'We were thinking of going further north this Christmas. A ski resort in Alberta has a special deal.'

Greta made a fist of her hand. The skin pulled and started bleeding again. It didn't seem like a foreign creature anymore. It seemed like just another boring injury, the kind old people are always getting from this or that.

'Are you sure you're all right, Mom?' said Nikki.

'I'm fine,' Greta said. 'I mean, I get a bit lonely –'

'I miss Dad too. But it's only been eighteen months. Have you tried any of those bereavement groups I found online?'

'No, no. You're right. I should try those groups.'

'Or I could look up some grief therapists in your area?'

Greta let her head drop forwards onto the car's hooter. The engine was off and no sound came out.

'Mom...?'

Greta reached into the well of the passenger seat for her bag. 'Can I read something to you, Nikki?'

'Sure, okay.'

Greta reworded the card slightly. '"Death can help shape and re-shape the family. It can be a link to new visions of being together." What d'you think of that?'

'What bull.'

'I agree.'

'Where did you read it?'

'In a paper given at the University of the Third Age.'

'I never knew you were going to U3A again, Mom! That's awesome!'

'But you said it was bull –'

'What talks are you attending?'

'Ancient Greece, Ancient Rome, the Persian Empire...'

Greta tried to think of more collapsed civilizations but then Nikki said, 'Mom, I'm going to have to go. I'm in the disabled toilet and someone's knocking.'

The disabled toilet. Clouds drifted over the sun and dulled the day's colours. 'Okay, well, sorry to have disturbed you at work.'

'It's all right, Mom. And great about U3A.'

'Thanks, Nikki.'

'We'll speak as usual on Sunday.'

'As usual. Bye Nikki.'

'Bye, Mom.'

*

Greta stared at the card she'd been keeping in her bag like a talisman these eighteen months. 'Bull,' she said to the card. 'Bull, bull, bull.'

She put it on the dashboard and turned the keys in the ignition. She felt shaky again, hungry. Usually she kept a small bag of peanuts and raisins in the glove compartment, but now she found just a dusty mint. She put it in her mouth anyway. How she wished she were a person whom grief had made thin and frail, who took

solace in high-minded things. She'd been trying
to be like that, to impress Nikki in that way. And
she'd been doing fairly well; yes, she'd been
doing pretty fine the last few years before Harold
died. Yet, as Greta drove back down the hill,
towards town, and then a bit further on up
another hill towards Fairview Gardens complex,
she knew that if he hadn't died, if she'd been
grieving anyone else, the high-mindedness
would have continued. It was something about
Harold's being gone specifically that made it
stop.

She put her foot down harder on the
accelerator; she smelled burning rubber and
closed the ventilator slats. With the drought, there
were more fires at the informal settlements; wild
paraffin blazes that razed twenty, thirty family
homes at a time. She would make a trip to the
church this weekend with some powdered beef
soup and cans of melon and fig jam and creamed
sweetcorn. Perhaps she'd take some of the clothes
and blankets from the kist too; it was time she got
rid of them.

When Greta arrived at Fairview Gardens
Complex, she braked. She sat for a moment
tapping the wheel. Then spontaneously, she
swung left down the road towards the creek.
When Harold was around, she would never have

kept Van Rensburg's card. Definitely wouldn't have tried to decipher inane advice from it.

At the bottom of the complex, the fumes seemed worse. Breathing through her mouth, Greta rounded the corner of Van Rensburg's cul-de-sac. His mustard Datsun was under the carport at the end of the road though there was no sign of his bicycle. She wondered if the Datsun had been his wife's as she parked behind it. She reached for the handbrake, but her fingers clutched empty air. She looked down. She'd been driving with it on all the while; the fumes had been her own brakepads burning out.

Opening the car door, she coughed; the smell was stronger outside, acrid. So much for coming here surreptitiously. She took her bag from the passenger seat and the card from the dashboard. *death as a part of what shapes and re-shapes the family... a link to new visions of being together.* 'Seriously?' Harold would've said, one eyebrow cocked. She'd have enjoyed telling him about returning the card; he used to take a mischievous pride in her most bolshie behaviour. Yet, as she marched up Van Rensburg's path, she was relieved not to have to tell Harold about the handbrake. He could be funny in that way: he'd prized their no-claims-bonus highly and wouldn't have found her carelessness amusing at all.

He probably wouldn't have been amused by the colourful gecko knocker on Van Rensburg's railway sleeper door either. His sense of humour hadn't extended to house building style: he liked the fact that all the homes in the complex were similar with normal front doors and conventional doorbells.

Greta stared at mister gecko's shiny black eyes. She quite liked him; he was arty but kind of cute. Still, she wasn't here to admire Van Rensburg's quirks. Resting her hands on her thighs, she bent down as low as she could go. She tried to see if the gap under his door was wide enough to slide the card through. Not quite sure, she was about to give the card a good, strong shove when the door slid away from her. Before her appeared a pair of scuffed brown leather shoes, their laces knotted in several places. 'Oh, hello,' said Van Rensburg.

She held the card behind her back as she straightened up.

He had his rucksack on one shoulder and a dove grey beret on his head.

'I was just...' She stopped.

She felt him waiting patiently.

She noticed that his entrance hall smelled delicately of jasmine rice. It brought back a distant idea she'd had as a teenager of starting a new life one day in Japan. To his left was a black lacquered cabinet with an underworld of mythological sea serpents carved into it.

'Would you like to come inside?' he said.

'No, no,' Greta said. 'You were on your way out.'

'Only to go and fill potholes.' His face was serious but his eyes smiled.

His mat said 'welcome' in what looked like all of the country's eleven official languages.

When he opened his door wider, she surreptitiously slipped the card back into her bag. She wiped her feet carefully on the mat. As she stumbled slightly over a small unseen step, he put out a hand.

Then, gently, he closed the heavy door behind her.

The Sweet Sop

Ingrid Persaud

IF IS CHOCOLATE YOU looking for, and I talking
real cheap, then you can't beat Golden MegaMart
Variety & Wholesale Ltd in Marabella. Think of
a Costco boil down small small but choke up
with goods from top to bottom. When me and
Moms had that holiday in Miami by her brother
we were always in Costco. But till they open a
Costco in Trinidad go by Golden MegaMart.
They does treat people real good. As soon as I
reach they know I want at least thirty jars of
Nutella chocolate spread. And don't play like you
giving me anything else. I tell them I have my
reasons and that is what I want. But they always
trying. Just last week you should hear them.

'Eh, Slim Man, we get a nice chocolate. It just
come out. Rocky Mallow Road. Why you don't
eat a good chocolate nah man instead of this
chocolate in a bottle?'

'I good.'

'Is Cadbury I talking about. Try one nah. On the house.'

'Look don't hurt me head with no foolishness. And hurry up. Man have taxi waiting.'

I never used to eat chocolate all the time so. If is anything, give me a pack of peanuts or green mango with salt and pepper. Anything salty and I in that. Everything changed when my old man Reggie died. Now the only thing I eat is sliced bread with Nutella. Moms think I am going mad. I might be going mad. That is a question for the doctor them to decide. But what is as true as Lara can play cricket is that I am getting fat. Man, let's give Jack his jacket. I am enormous.

Computer work like I have mean you don't need to leave the house. In fact, most of the people I work for operating the same way rather than in an office set up. To stop me and Moms getting all up in each other's business, I turned the garage into a studio apartment as soon as I started working. I have my own toilet and bath and a small kitchen with a fridge. She is in the house proper but this way me and Moms don't have to bounce up every day. I am not a man to take more than two-three little drink but you see that woman. Ah lord. When she start up with she stupidness I does want to take a rum straight from the bottle. Is always the same tune. Victor, this bread and chocolate thing is your father fault, God rest he soul. You should have followed my example and don't have nothing to do with he. One minute you was a good-looking, normal, young man and then that worthless devil sit on your head. Now look at you. You is one big booboloops. You forget how to reach the gym? I don't understand what happen to you. You don't go out. You only home eating this bread and chocolate morning, noon and night. Chocolate and bread, bread and chocolate, chocolate and bread. Watch me. Your heart can't carry this size. Keep up this madness and you go be using a plot in Paradise Cemetery before me.

In a way Moms have a point. Is only after Reggie passed away that things got real dread. They say the leukaemia take him. That is part of the truth. I know the other part. The truth about what happened the night Reggie died is something I taking with me to the grave. You have to understand that I didn't know Reggie much at all until the year before he passed. Growing up I could count the number of times I saw him on one hand. Somehow he used to know when big things were happening and show up. Like when I did Common Entrance, he reached in the school and gave me a blue note.

One hundred dollars.

He had on shades and I didn't make him out. Then loud loud he was saying, 'But eh, eh, Victor, how you don't recognise your own father?'

I remember that because the whole class must be hear him and know all my business.

Another time he reached by the house after I got confirmed in the Cathedral of Our Lady of Perpetual Help. Church not my thing but Moms say while I living under she roof I will learn some righteousness. Moms spot Reggie by the gate first. She shouted out for me to go and see what my father want but don't let that stinking man put a foot in this house. Then she bawl out that if he ask for me tell him to haul his ass. That kind of bad mind was not Christian but I wasn't saying boo. I am not that brave or that stupid. Reggie must have heard her because he stayed on the road. He gave me two hundred dollars and asked me how my studies going. According to Reggie, his family had brains in it except the brains run zigzag. He sure I get what he miss out. I think he was hoping I would become a big shot lawyer or doctor.

After that it was nearly six years I had to wait to hear from him. Don't ask me what have him so busy for all that time. Moms let out one long steups when she find out he get in touch. It seems the man sick bad and wanted to see me.

'Wash your foot and jump in if you want,' she said. 'You see me, as far as that man concern, I will never forgive his whore-mongering and I will never ever forget what he do. He leave when you was three months. Three months. And now the Lord calling him home he want to spend time with you? Shame on he.'

It was my Auntie's mouth that opened and made the story jump out. Moms found Reggie with the neighbour's daughter and threw him out then and there. And Moms, being from Tobago, is not like she had much family to help her out. That is how strong she is. The young lady in question is none other than the woman with the bakery on Mucurapo Street. People say she does make nice Hops bread and she currants-roll sweet too bad. Me? I would rather starve than put my big toe in there. Mind you, whatever went on between she and Reggie didn't last. She ended up with Mr Louchoo and that is how she get bakery. As for Reggie, he married to one good-looking lady name Kim. Go by Kenny Khan Bookstore and Variety Shop – is downstairs the big, green building in Cross Crossing. Kim is some kind of manager there.

The same Auntie who buss the mark is the one who tell me not to mind Moms and go see Reggie on he sick bed. If I don't go, and the man dead, I might end up regretting that we didn't talk. Not that he look overjoyed to see me when I reach. He was lying down on the couch. Reggie was never a big man but now you could see all his bones jooking out. His legs thin like two pencils and his face hollow. I said 'I heard he not doing any more treatment.'

'What I going to do that for? I have enough poison in my body.'

'But it could make you better.'

'How you know that? Like you is a doctor now?'

He had to stop and take deep breaths.

'Look I tell you already. I done with all that hospital thing. They ain't even sure it would help me now. Gopaul luck is not Seepaul luck. I take that treatment and I could end up seeing more trouble.'

Kim was nice. She looked a good bit younger than Reggie. What woman does see in old man I don't know. She claimed she was always telling Reggie to invite me home by them. Reggie was right there watching me but he didn't say much. I tried to ask him how he was doing and if there was anything I could help with. All I got back were gruff grunts and yes or no answers. After a while he ignored me completely and put on the sports channel. I stayed and watched TV with him for a good hour then I told them I have to make tracks before it get too dark. Kim gave me sweet bread straight from the oven to carry home. She say tell your mother is Kim sent it because the two of we don't have no quarrel. I was by the front door before Reggie turned off the TV and looked up.

'So when you coming back to see me?'

I moved the bag with the sweet bread from one hand to the next.

'I might pass next week.'

'Don't give me a six for a nine. I is a dying man.'

'You go see me.'

'Make sure. I go be waiting.'

If Kim wasn't right there I think I would have let go two bad words in he tail.

He waiting.

He.

Waiting.

Lord Jesus, don't get me started. But then I remembered that he is on his way out. If this heaven and hell thing is correct, then he going where no amount of air conditioning will keep him from burning up. Things have a way of levelling out.

The only slight problem with the levelling out business was that Reggie decided he was going to take his own cool time to pass. I ended up having to go Saturday after Saturday. If I didn't go he would get Kim to call and ask me to come over. They don't have much help so Kim needed me. Poor thing. She was either working or looking after him without a free five minutes. Reggie didn't like nothing better than when was only me and he. He must have been an army general in a past life.

'Victor, bring juice.'

I would bring the juice.

'Oh lord this thing freezing cold. That is what you go bring for me?'

Two minutes later he would be hungry. Kim always left something on the stove – a little stew chicken or she nice corn soup.

'I don't care what she cook. I don't want it. I want a boil egg and a piece of bread. You could boil egg? Don't make the egg hard, hard.'

Of course the egg was always too soft or too hard. More than once, after I put it on a plate, he would push it aside claiming he was too tired to eat. It was not tiredness. It was bad mind stopping him. He enjoyed having me waiting on him like he was the king of Trinidad. A favourite of his was to ask for a glass of water and no matter how much water was in the glass he would complain and make me take it back.

'Like you want to drown me? Give me a glass with half of that.'

Or I might get:

'Well I never see more. You put water in this glass? Like water lock off?'

But you had to feel sorry for the man. Restless and in pain, Reggie would be walking up and down from the living room to the kitchen and outside patio. I never knew where I should be. To him I was always in the wrong place. I remember a day he was watching a test match – Pakistan v West Indies – and I was sitting on a chair to the side. All I did was lean forward to check out *The Guardian* newspaper and he started carrying on.

'I know your father is not a glass maker so move from in front the TV.'

Another time his bad temper was for a bracelet I had on. He took one look and decided that it was a ladies' band.

'I didn't know you is a batty man.'

I bit my lips and stayed cool.

'Everybody wearing bracelet like this. Is the fashion.'

'Well monkey see, monkey do.'

I good with that. Here you can still get locked up for being with a man. So, if people call you a dotish monkey, take it.

For a whole six months Reggie carried on with his army general thing barking orders at me even though he weakie weakie. I could not tell you when last he even walked outside the house. But the man still had fight in his spirit. He would point his bony finger in my face and say all you will have to wait. Is not time yet for Mahadeo Funeral Home. I kept wondering how long he would drag this out and why I was such a jackass to let myself get dragged in.

Then one Saturday he asked me to go buy him a chocolate. He was feeling for a Fruit and Nut bar. Now this was a man with stage four of the big C, plus high pressure and even higher sugar. I knew Kim didn't keep anything like sweet biscuits or chocolates in the house. But Major Reggie wasn't backing down.

'Victor, I am dying. You hear that? I having to eat bread that the Devil he-self knead. A lil' chocolate is all I begging for.'

What to do? You should have seen how he licked down that chocolate. Half a big bar was gone before he stopped to breathe.

'How your mother?'

I nodded and made a noise to confirm she was fine.

'Well you must tell she hello from me.'

I nodded again. His brains clearly not working

good or else he would have known not to be
sending Moms no hello.

'Your mother ain't easy, yes. She ever learn to
cook?'

It was best to keep my mouth shut.

Reggie made sucking noises as he tried to
clear the bits of dried fruit stuck between his
teeth.

'You want me to tell you what really went on
between your mother and me?'

I looked up slightly. He was eyeing me good.

'You mother didn't understand that when you
married you can't keep running by this one and
that one. What go on in a man house should stay
in a man house. But your mother was always
broadcasting we business to the marish and the
parish. And when I tell she anything she would
start up one set of quarrelling.'

I swallowed hard and looked down at my
sneakers.

'Two bo-rat can't live in one hole. That is the
truth.'

He chomped on a block of chocolate but just
because his mouth was full didn't stop him from
running it.

'Is a good thing I get out from under that
woman and all she foolishness.'

I took out my phone and started checking

emails. Reggie gave a little, mocking laugh.

'Alright Victor, don't listen. Believe what you want. But remember, you only know chapter. You don't know the book.'

He scrunched up the purple chocolate wrapper and handed it to me.

'Take that with you when you going. Kim be real vex if she know you feeding me chocolate.'

No joke, some days I wished he would hurry up and die.

Instead, the memory of chocolate made the man crazy to see me. I became Reggie's dealer. A voice on the phone would whisper, 'Two Kit Kat,' and hang up. The bathroom was a favourite hiding place. I could hear water falling in the background and then his voice hissing, 'Snickers. King-size.' After a few weeks he say he easing back on the sugar so he only want Bournville Dark Chocolate. Who he fooling? Two days later he begging me please bring a Galaxy Caramel. He can't take the bitter taste. Then he had worries about the ingredients. I should bring something organic. When I told him the organic chocolate was real money he said forget that. We don't know for sure if organic better and besides he going to dead soon.

This secret chocolate handover was our special sin. Everybody know that a little secret-sinning sweet too bad. If you don't agree I know you lying through your teeth. In them sinning moments Reggie softened, forgot his constant pain and forgot to fight the big C. He even forgot to fight me. Plus something else happened. He would be eating a Bounty or Hershey's Kisses, and just so he would start giving me the lowdown on growing up in the countryside and leaving school with only a couple subjects. His parents thought he was a joker with no brains and he believed them. He said for years he felt like he lost his soul. But an uncle took him in and got him a place at the technical school in San Fernando. Reggie said that was a debt he could never fully repay. Since then he never wanted for work.

A Mars bar (super-size) helped Reggie take his mind off the reality that he was living full time in the bedroom now. Instead he talked about long time. He told me about meeting Moms – a story she never told me. Back in the day, Moms was working as a receptionist in an office he was rewiring.

'In them days it didn't have no Tinder hook-up business like what all you young people does do.'

He laughed at my shock.

'You didn't think I know what does go on these days?'

Reggie used to wait at the bus stand when Moms finished work 4 o'clock. They used to stop at Dairy Queen for ice cream – vanilla for her, chocolate for him. Reggie would take a chance and hold her hand or play footsie under the table. But he said they should never have married. Somebody should have talked some sense in them because they were too young.

'Victor, that was a case of sweet in goat mouth but sour in the bam bam. One minute is love like dove but, before you could turn around twice, we was ready to kill one another.'

I got up and asked if he wanted some water to wash down the Mars bar but he was far away.

Half hour later, when I was leaving, he still seemed lost.

'Reggie, I heading out now.'

He looked up, his hollow face creased up with pain.

'You could call me Dad you know.'

I breathed in hard. Reggie looked at the wall opposite then back at me.

'You know, I wanted to ask you something. Why your mother never married again, boy?'

I shrugged.

'It's probably too late for she now. Mind you, she does still go to church every Sunday?'

'Yeah.'

'It have plenty randy old timers that does go church and they not going to praise the Lord.'

By now I was helping Reggie bathe or cutting up his food and bribing him with the chocolate. While he nibbled on a Twix I told him about what I did and how I liked being my own boss. He didn't understand computers and coding – not that he let that stop him.

'Victor, it don't matter if you does sweep the road or if you is prime minister. Once you could say, yes, I doing my best. Once you could say that, you go be a happy man.'

I was home eating left over macaroni pie and baked chicken when Kim called. The doctor had left having told Reggie that he should be in hospital or he would die quickly and in real pain. Reggie's response had been to throw two cuss words at the doctor. He was not budging. Kim was sobbing and begging me to speak with him. I understood that this was a moment to come out strong. This was a Lindt moment. Even his wilfulness would melt with this fancy Swiss chocolate.

From the time Reggie refused the Lindt Excellence Extra Creamy chocolate bar I knew he was ready to close his eyes for good.

'Reggie, you don't know what you missing.'

He shut his eyes tight. It looked like he was trying not to cry.

'Why you never once call me Dada or Daddy or something so?'

I felt like someone had pelted a cricket ball straight at my head and knocked me out. What was I supposed to say? Should I lie so the man could rest his soul in peace? What about me? Would my soul rest peacefully?

After one time is another and from that day Reggie went down fast fast. I tried giving him Nestle Butterfinger but he refused it. I brought him Crunchie. Same thing. I broke up a bar of Oh Henry to see if he would eat even a little piece but nothing doing. I tried Smarties, Milky Way, Aero, Rolo, Charles Chocoloco, Twix and some others I can't even remember the name of now. If they were selling it, I bought it, but not one of them made Reggie even give a smile.

In his final days I was practically living in their small house, sleeping on the couch. He wasn't talking much. That did not stop him letting me know if he wanted something. Mr Army General was still there. I might be checking Facebook on my phone and suddenly feel a bony finger jab my leg. A hand taking an invisible cup to his lips meant bring water now. A pat of the mattress meant he was fed up on that side and I better turn him. There were no more stories about life in Cedros and running away from school to dip in the sea. I asked him to tell me again how he was caught thiefing Julie mango from a neighbour's tree. Or the time he get licks for taking his father bicycle and going to a party when he should have been home sleeping. I wanted him to tell me again how he has only one picture of me – a bald baby in a sailor outfit. Tell me again how that picture never leave his mash-up wallet for the past twenty-four years.

The few times he did speak it was only about dying. He said he couldn't talk to Kim because she was still hoping he would live to enjoy Christmas and the parang season. Reggie didn't have the heart to say that this year she making black cake, sorrel and punch de crème by she-self. He begged to know if death itself, when you are actually about to die, if that was more pain. I lied as best I could.

He was always behind me to help him pass quickly. The first time he said it I wasn't sure what he wanted.

'You want some more painkillers Reggie?'

'I want you to mash up all and give me with some water.'

'You can't swallow?'

'No monkey.'

'I can't give you more than the dose.'

'Why? I begging you. Please. Let me go in peace.'

'You will go in peace.'

Tears started dripping down his cheeks.

'How you know that? You eh see how I suffering here? You should be helping me.'

'Then let me carry you to the hospital.'

We had that same talk so many times I lost track. I ain't lying. Seeing Reggie slipping away slow slow, and in so much pain, made me feel sick too. But life is life. He was asking me to make a jail for murder. Even if nobody ever find out I had to ask myself who I was doing this for. You know how many times I wished I could tell people my father dead? When you young that sounds cool instead of telling people my father ups and gone he way. But he not dead. He dying but he not dead and I didn't know how long this dying thing could stretch out for. Whole day, whole night he was restless and crying. You know what it is to hear a big man bawling all the time?

Yet, in those hard, final days, chocolate Reggie sometimes slipped back in the groove.

'Boy, Victor.'

I bent close.

'I feel I go be the next Lazarus. What you think?'

He gave a feeble smile.

'I go dead and then bam, get up from this bed and live out my days cool as anything.'

The doctor came to house a few times. He left strong pain tablets while still telling Reggie to go into hospital. Reggie said if anybody wanted him to leave 30B Hibiscus Drive they would have to wait till he in a coffin.

One night I was taking a sleep on the chair next to his bed when Reggie started jabbing my leg.

'Water?'

He shook his head then whispered.

'I was dreaming about carnival.'

'You were playing mas?'

'Nah. I don't think so. I was hearing a Mighty Sparrow calypso.'

'Which one?'

He started to hum, 'All them Tobago gyal…'

He coughed.

'Sweet sweet sweet like a butterball. La la la la la.'

I joined in.

'Anytime they call, I have to crawl, like a old football, I rolling straight to my Tobago gyal.'

I squeezed his hand.

'Rest. Is the middle of the night.'

He began to cry softly.

'I can't take this no more. No more.'

I got up. I could see myself going to the kitchen, like I was following my body. I watched as I mashed up every painkiller I could find with a rolling pin. In a cup I mixed the white powder with Nutella.

He was still crying when I followed myself back into the bedroom.

'Have some Nutella.'

He shook his head.

I took his hand and looked him straight in the eye.

'Eat some chocolate nah.'

He didn't move.

'Daddy, is what you asked for.'

His eyes opened wide wide and I felt his hand squeeze mine.

'Thank you, son.'

Reggie blinked and more tears spilled down his cheeks.

'Go catch a sleep on the couch, Victor. The longest day have an end.'

At the door I turned around for one last look. My dad was licking chocolate off the spoon bringing ease for him and, in time, for me.

The Minutes

Nell Stevens

1.

WE ARE WAITING FOR Peter to get here so the meeting can start. There's a bad atmosphere in the room – something between Kat and Adam, I think – and I've volunteered to take the minutes so I can keep my head down, typing.

Location: Kat's apartment, a low-ceilinged new-build place in Peckham, where everything feels too close together and tuneless singing strains through the walls: the neighbours are holding a prayer circle. Occasional shouts of 'Amen!' and 'Praise Jesus!' punctuate the droning.

Present: Kat, on the floor, her legs stretched out under the glass coffee table and her elbows resting atop it; Diya, curled up on the sofa, reading; Adam, at the main table, flicking through his phone and pretending not to be furious about whatever it is that Kat has done or not done that he is furious about. Now Peter has arrived, and is already talking too loudly, and everyone is gathering around the coffee table. Diya pours wine into tumblers. Kat spreads her hands over the surface of the glass, as though she's trying to smooth out a crease, and says, 'Let's get into it, then.' When she shifts her legs, a flake of mud falls away from the sole of her shoe, like a stray puzzle piece. The meeting starts.

Apologies – or rather, conspicuous lack of apology – from: You.

Item 1: the dismantling of our exhibition of squatters' art. The show is housed in an abandoned building with boarded up windows – it used to be a pub – and the plan was for the exhibition to be ousted, forcibly, by the landlord, hopefully in the presence of a photographer, and that the record of this eviction would then form the basis of a subsequent display. Except that the landlord has failed to notice the presence of the squatters' art in his property for two months now, so the anticipated expulsion has not taken place, and we all have more pressing things to do than continue to man it, especially since everyone who was ever going to visit came to the private view, and hasn't returned. Term is about to start: the final term of our final year of university; we need to spend more time in the library and less time supervising the exhibition. We will have to take the art down ourselves.

'Or we could just leave it there,' says Diya, 'and see what happens to it over time. It might fall down, or get stolen, and we can keep a record, photograph it, the death of art.'

Peter objects to the concept of treating art as disposable.

Adam agrees with Peter, and says we should at least notify the artists that they can collect their work.

Diya: 'We could ask if they were willing to donate the works to a project examining artistic decay. What happens to a painting that nobody looks at? That sort of thing.'

Peter, glancing across at me, at my fingers on the keyboard: 'Diya's suggestions are noted in the minutes. Thanks Diya.'

I nod and underline Diya's original thought about the death of art. Diya sighs and a storm is brewing, an argument about the boys talking over the girls, dismissing our contributions (and I'm noting this down, too, then switch *boys* to *men* and *girls* to *women*, then back again because it seemed pretentious and not particularly accurate) and it seems extraordinary that the boys, the men, the boys, whatever, can't feel it, or don't care.

Your absence is unfortunate. Without you we all feel sheepish and self-conscious and therefore more irritable. Just a bunch of students with nothing better to do than – what was it Leah said before she left? – 'Pretend that affected stunts and the parroting of half-baked political ideologies is a valuable artistic contribution'. This is why we were all so pleased when you turned up at one of our meetings. Leah, a founding member, had lost patience and abandoned ship, leaving the rest of us feeling rudderless, suddenly unsure what the hell we thought we were doing. Or that was how I felt, and guessed the others did. Then you came along, and things felt clear again. We could never admit it, but it adds gravitas, it protects us against criticisms like Leah's, to have a bona fide local on our team. *We are a group of young artists based in South London, with an interest in urban exploration, subversive design, art as activism and supporting marginalised communities.* Without you, we are idealistic, self-aggrandising, pretentious. With you, we're endorsed: the real deal.

(Your absence is a shame, too, because I like to catch your eye sometimes during meetings like these, and feel that we're laughing at the same thing, that you and I both know this is all a bit ridiculous, the death of art, the un-evicted squatters' exhibition, but that it's moving, too, how much we all care, how, at the bottom of everything, we really do think art saves lives. So little difference between us, really, and the faithful praying on the other side of the wall.)

Item 2, which is the only other item, is what we can do to protest, or at least bear critical witness to, the demolition of the Waderley Tower Block by the roundabout near the university.

Peter glances around at all of us and then asks, sharply, where you are.

*

A fact lost on nobody: You used to live in Waderley. You grew up on the thirteenth floor, knew its views, smells, the various vibrations of footsteps in the stairwell according to which storey they were passing. It's embarrassing to say it but I was shocked – first shocked, and then, perhaps worse, impressed – when, as we passed the tower block on the bus one day, not long after we first met, you pointed up to some indeterminate point on the building's flank and said, 'That's my dad's place.'

The building looked so hostile; you are always so warm.

They've razed everything around the tower already. The Waderley Estate used to border the roundabout on all sides, a big grey nest around a big grey egg. Now, the other buildings are gone: the long concrete walkways, the walls polka-dotted with satellite dishes. Too much crime and not enough community spirit, the council thought: *An area of extremely high social disadvantage.* Too expensive to renovate, to coax back into respectability. Better, they decided, to reduce it to rubble, and then to nothing; to build a shopping centre on top of where it used to be, and luxury flats on top of the shopping centre, and the university was thrilled by the plans and did nothing to stop them. All that remains, now, is the tower: a solitary watchman presiding over all this empty space, foundations gaping in the ground and scaffolding already going up.

Our group has discussed the demolition before. I've noticed a certain deferral to you when we talk about it. We have already done our best to prevent the eviction of residents, have unfurled all the usual banners – '*PEOPLE BEFORE PROFIT, RENT IS THEFT*' – have written blog posts and erected a petition stand outside the library and started hashtags. But the people are gone, now. Your father has been rehoused in an outer borough. The windows are blank, and there are loops of barbed wire strung all over the walls like the Christmas lights around the university buildings, though it is January, now, and they should have been taken down.

That day on the bus, as we juddered around an assault course of roadworks and you directed my eyes up at the tower, I was so interested in you: in the fact that you grew up right here in this place that is now my home, too, but which will always seem strange and bleak to me, and that from here you went so far away, to America, to get your Masters; that you came back to do your PhD at our university, and for some reason wanted to spend time with us, with me, with a bunch of undergraduates avoiding studying for our final exams by littering the environs of the campus with art and slogans; that you are receptive and helpful when I rant about my classes, my teachers, my essays and then afterwards I'll check my phone and see that while we were talking, you were also posting a multi-tweet thread about the facility of Komodo dragons to have virgin births. How do you do that, I want to know; how do you live in all these worlds at once? You have tens of thousands of Twitter followers and they all seem as fascinated by you as I am.

Soon after you told me about Waderley, one of my housemates took acid and set fire to the kitchen. You and I decided to live together. We moved into a flat by Burgess Park with one bedroom, and we took turns sleeping in the bed.

*

I am supposed to be taking the minutes, and if I'd been doing a good job of it, I'd be able to clear up the dispute that has arisen, now, about whose idea it was to engineer something that has been named, instantly, 'the Ascension of Waderley.' But my mind wandered – I was thinking about you, about the flat, about whether you mentioned this morning that you wouldn't be at the meeting – and suddenly Diya and Kat are both shouting at Peter and Adam, and Peter and Adam are leaning back, arms crossed, smirking at each other, and all I can do is type frantically and catch nobody's eye.

Here's what I've been aware of happening, at the edges of my attention: someone saying, 'Imagine what it would look like if, when the demolition began, the bricks went up instead of down. Imagine if it looks like Waderley's ascending.'

Someone else – a male voice? – 'Think of it this way: if Waderley were an animal, it would be a pigeon.' And then, somehow, a collective vision of Waderley filled with pigeons, the birds the exact colour of its walls, and the dust billowing outwards as the building starts to collapse, the birds surging up so it looks as though the bricks had sprouted wings and are flying away. The Ascension of Waderley.

Diya: It is unacceptable for you to take credit for this.

Peter: What exactly do you think you have contributed, here?

Me: It would kill the pigeons.

Kat: She has contributed the idea, the whole thing.

'It would kill the pigeons,' I say. 'The pigeons would just explode.'

★

My stomach drops when I think about your hands – as though I'm a child in the back of a car accelerating joyfully over a bump in the road – the way you fold them around your knees when you're talking to me. Lately you've been doing that – talking to me, holding your knees – while I'm in the bath. You come in and sit on the toilet while I splash about. The air is steamy and you wave your hand in front of your face, as though someone were smoking upwind, which I take as a sort of jokey criticism of my profligate use of hot water. Then you lean back, clutch your legs and tell me about your day.

You are writing a thesis about Walter

Benjamin's *Arcades Project*, but most of your time is spent wandering around the city trying to find a place where you can work. There's never anywhere. The cafés are crowded with students and prams. The pubs are full of men who ask why you're alone. The library, you say, is oppressive: so many books crammed on the shelves, so many people jostling for desk space. You share oddly-angled photos of your workplaces, your failing-to-workplaces, with your followers online. The updates come hourly, sometimes minute by minute. You'd forgotten how it is in London, you tweet, after living in America: how impossible it is to find a place to sit down.

Last week: 'Can I come in?' you asked, because you always do, as you pushed the door and slid through. 'Guess what I did today?'

I turned over onto my front, splashing a bit, and the squeak of my skin against the wall of the tub sounded sort of obscene. 'What did you do?'

I thought you would say what you normally say: 'I tried to get work done in the British Library, in the Starbucks by Borough Station, in the Trafalgar Arms.'

Instead: 'I went to Waderley.' In your mouth the word Waderley sounds different, less reverent than when the rest of us say it.

I pictured you standing on the pavement,

staring up at the tower. People would have been annoyed at you blocking the walkway; cyclists would have dinged their bells as they swerved around you on the new bike lane. There had been no photo posted of the tower, no tweet about it, and it seemed therefore like privileged information. I waited for you to tell me how you felt, seeing the upright corpse of your old home.

To sound encouraging but not patronising, I just said, 'Uh huh?'

You paused, pulling your knees closer, peering over the top of them at your toes curled round the toilet seat. 'I found a way in.'

'In?' I said. 'Like, inside in?'

You nodded. 'There's a way into the building round the back. There are some security cameras but I don't think they're on. All those signs about guard dogs are just for show. I cut through some wire. The back door into the building, where the boiler and the pipes are, it's just open. I just walked right in.'

'It's not safe,' I said. 'It might not be structurally sound.' I felt a pang of irritation. I was annoyed to think of you doing this, though I had no evidence the building was dangerous, no genuine fear other than something vague and selfish I couldn't name.

Your eyes were wide. You were speaking quickly.

'We should do something in the tower,' you said. 'We should break in again, all of us, and do something before the demolition. Something big. Peter will love it. He'll finally get to be like those people who climbed the Shard. Or the ones who broke into Aldgate tube at the royal wedding. We'll all go in and we'll find a way to say goodbye to Waderley, something beautiful.'

'What?' I asked.

'I don't know,' you said. 'Make some art. A bigger explosion than the actual explosion. I don't know.'

'They got ASBOs, those Aldgate tube people,' I say. 'They weren't allowed to talk to each other for ten years.'

I turned over. Bath water splashed onto your leg. I sank down so that my ears were underwater, and my own voice sounded explosive in my head when I said, 'Ten years. Imagine not talking for ten years.' I came up and studied your expression.

'We won't have to do that,' you said, and I felt soft again, warm towards you. 'We won't get caught.'

I flicked some water at your face and you crowed. You bent over the bath and splashed some back at me, which made me kick and at that point you were half-soaked already and we were both laughing and you jumped in on top of me, fully clothed. Water got into my mouth and made me splutter. You wriggled and kicked. Half the contents of the tub ended up on the floor and the neighbour on the other side of the wall thumped it a few times until we shut up. A bigger explosion than the actual explosion. We lay still, tangled limbs and dripping hair, and we panted and listened to the leftover quiet in the room.

So it occurs to me now that perhaps it was my idea: the Ascension of Waderley. Or at least, the filtering of your idea, through me, into the conversation, into the minutes.

2.

Back at Kat's place for another meeting. There was a party here last weekend, and leftover detritus makes it feel as though we are posing for one of the photographs in the squatters' art exhibition. It's cold; I'm wrapped in a blanket that was thrown over the side of the sofa. The laptop I'm typing on nestles against the wool, which smells strongly of cheap aftershave and makes me think of the boys I fell in love with in my first year, the exaggerated way they used to move their shoulders as they walked, as though they could power their legs from the neck down. They were so impressive to me: solid and desirable. It seems longer than two years ago that I felt that way about them.

You are here, now, though you're busy on your phone and won't look at me.

'We've got the pumps and the balloon samples,' Peter says.

'Uh huh?' you say, as though he were telling this to you alone, and I want you to be livelier, to be more pleased, because who are we doing this for, why are we doing this, if not for you, if not to please you?

There has been a flurry of messages on the group chat since the last meeting, and the Waderley plan has morphed into something more concrete and – slightly, so slightly it seems, still, like a punchline to a joke I didn't hear – more realistic.

You: 'So just to get this straight, you want to fill the building with pigeons.'

Peter: 'Yes.'

Kat: 'The Ascension of Waderley.'

You: 'But the pigeons would just die.'

Me: 'That's what I said.'

You: 'They'd just get blown up with everything else.'

Me: 'Exactly.'

You: 'I've seen video of tower blocks being demolished. They fire a shot at first, to scare off birds in the building – and what you're suggesting is that we lock pigeons in a room so they can't escape, and they'll hear that warning shot and start to panic, but they won't be able to get out, it'll be chaos and feathers and screeching and terror and they'll be throwing themselves at the windows, and then the building will explode and that will have been their final living moment.'

Peter: 'It's unclear that the birds would die.'

Me: 'They'll definitely die.'

You: 'Pigeons can detect sounds at lower frequencies than humans. They can hear volcanos and storms from hundreds of miles away.'

Peter: 'Ok.'

Adam: 'If we ascertain where, exactly, the explosives will be placed in the building, we can ensure the birds are far away from the sites of the explosions, and just escape when the building begins to disintegrate.'

You: 'Why not use balloons.'

Diya: 'Balloons?'

You: 'Grey helium balloons.'

Me: 'Yes, grey helium balloons.'

Conversation moved on to the practicalities of balloons, of whether the force of the explosion would burst them, and you uttered the words that stopped everyone in their tracks – 'as a former resident of the tower' – and you said that if even one grey balloon survived the explosion, if even one brick appeared to float upwards when the building sank down, you'd consider the installation a success. 'Plans are afoot for a Waderley send off (/up)' you tweeted, and I was proud to know what you meant.

So now here we are. Present: you, me, everyone else. Apologies from no one.

There's a sort of fizzing energy between us that comes from the aftermath of an argument, a new shared purpose, though you seem somewhat immune from it, slumped in the corner: you're frowning, thumbs darting across the bottom half of your phone. We have hired helium pumps from a party shop near Peter's house. Diya and I spent several hours sourcing and ordering various grey balloons online, which Adam now spreads out across the coffee table, an interior designer's swatch of Waderley shades: light, dark, metallic, dull, marbled, translucent, mauve, pigeon-toned. Beside them, Adam places images of the tower. We blow up balloons and compare them to the pictures.

'What do you think?' I ask you, and you just shrug, slide your phone into your pocket, as though even that is boring you now. I check my timeline: you've been arguing with a stranger about whether 'gotten' can be used in British English. 'Forgotten,' you have tweeted. 'Begotten. Misbegotten. Ungotten. Gotten.'

You have been different these past few days: I don't want to say *avoiding me* but it does feel that way. I've been frantically lonely, listening out for your key in the door of the flat. I miss you. Perhaps it has been longer that you've been like this: a couple of weeks, since the bath thing.

We narrow it down to two shades of balloons and take a vote.

★

Yesterday you gave a lecture to my Criticism and Theory class. The timetable read 'BENJAMIN LECTURE' with no speaker listed. I had mentioned to you that it was happening, because I thought you'd be interested, and you had nodded and not let on that you'd be the one giving it. Then, on the day, there you were, walking out onto the platform at the front of the room. You tapped the keyboard and the screen above you opened its eye. Black background, white words: THE WORK OF ART IN THE AGE OF MECHANICAL REPRODUCTION and your name underneath in lower case.

The next slide was a photograph of flowers – bulbous crystal vase on a grey surface, petals white and pink and red, the leaves and stalks in muted greens, the palette of something Dutch and old –

and underneath it, 'A still from 'Big Bang' (2006), Ori Gersht'. You pressed a key and the picture began to move. The vase exploded in slow motion. Red petals splintering out like fragments of coloured glass. Next: video of the video, the same bouquet exploding, playing on several stacked screens running up the side of a tall building. Next: quote from Ori Gersht: 'When the explosion happened, you had the sense that that entire building was collapsing.'

Prickle of sweat between my skin and the collar of my shirt. I felt as though this was all for me, supposed to hit me right between the eyes. Then: 'What is the difference,' you said, 'between a painting, and a photograph of a painting? Between a vase of flowers exploding and a video of a vase of flowers exploding? Between a video of a vase of flowers exploding and a video of a video of a vase of flowers exploding?'

Afterwards, when you had slunk off the stage and we were filing out of the theatre, I felt swelled up inside with pride, fullest of grey balloons, because you had been so casually clever up there and because I knew you. Or, if I didn't really know you, then because you were my person.

I got home later that day to find you eating sunflower seeds at the kitchen table. It was mid-afternoon, not dark yet but thinking about it, the sky just beginning to congeal into something murky, and I was so happy to see you: tangible you who crunches things between your teeth, not the far-off, cool-edged you who had given the lecture, or the cypher of yourself offering opinions on the internet. 'I liked your lecture,' I said. You stood up and the legs of your chair scraped against the floor. You walked to the window. 'Nobody likes lectures,' you said. The tree outside was waving its branches behind your head and it looked for a moment as though you were tangled in it.

'Everyone wanted to be you,' I said and you gave me a look of such offended pity, sorry and wounded and sour.

'Oh don't start acting your age,' you said, and spat out a striped shell into the palm of your hand.

'I'm interested in those oppositions of attraction and repulsion,' said Ori Gersht, in a slide from the lecture, 'and how the moment of destruction in the exploding flowers becomes for me the moment of creation.'

*

The meeting has run long and everyone is tired, losing focus. Peter is playing with the helium pumps, practising filling balloons. He's waving them in your direction, saying, 'This colour is right, right? You're sure this is right?' You're leaning away from him as though you can smell his breath. Each time you move back, you edge closer to me, and I move my leg out from under the blanket, and wonder whether you'll touch it.

Diya bats a balloon away from her face. 'The demolition is scheduled for noon on Friday,' she says. She points to one of the photos of the building. 'We know there will be simultaneous explosions on different floors, and our best guess is here, and here, and here.'

And this is the plan: we will meet at two a.m. on the day of the demolition, take the route that you have already found into Waderley, and divide ourselves into two groups. One set will go to the thirteenth floor, roughly half way up, use the key you still have to access your father's place, and fill it with balloons. The other will go to the very top floor, force entry into one of the flats there and do the same. Since we don't know exactly where the explosives will be, this seems our safest bet.

'Does everyone know what they're supposed to be doing?' says Peter.

I draw the blanket closer around me and write that the meeting has ended before it has technically ended. My outstretched leg is like a question mark on the floor. You haven't touched it.

It strikes me that everyone in this room is in love with you.

3.

Location: the barred entrance to the abandoned tower. Waderley is looming blackly overhead, dark lump against velvety, light-polluted sky. Everything seems flat in the streetlight; your face in particular looks blank. Darting red edge of Diya's cigarette. We are all wearing hoods. It is Friday. It is 1.59 a.m.

Present, now: all of us except Peter, who texted saying he'd been 'held up' and telling us to go on without him, which means he got drunk and/or lucky and either way is in bed with no intention of getting out of it. Without him – his unquestioning confidence in his own right to take charge – we're all looking at you, waiting for you to tell us what to do.

'Ok?' says Diya and you mutter, 'Ok.'

Nobody seems to want to move. You say, 'Ok,' again. I take a deep breath and the smell is damp leaves and petrol and the washing powder you use which now I use as well. A motorbike speeds around the roundabout. High-pitched mosquito whine.

You turn to the wire fence that divides the world from Waderley, running your fingers along it, feeling for the break you made before. The wire jangles under your palms.

Diya: 'Where did you cut it?'

You: 'I'm looking. Give me a second.'

Adam: 'I can't see a hole. They repaired it.'

You (mystified): 'They never repair anything.'

But the hole you made is gone, and Kat is fishing wire-cutters out of Adam's bag and handing them to you. You don't react for a moment, just stare at the mesh, and then you take them. You open the jaws of the cutter and close them. You look as though you are gardening, trimming a hedge, but I can smell the metal. You make cuts. The sharp edges of the broken wires catch light from the road. A car hoots its horn but none of us turn to see if it was directed at us; when nothing else happens, you continue to work. A flap of mesh is loose, now. You peel it back as though it were a page of newspaper, and duck through. After you: Kat, Adam, Diya and then me. On the other side, even though it can't be, everything seems quieter.

We file around to the back of the building, moving close to the wall. Security cameras, lights not blinking. I have two of the helium pumps in my backpack and they're clanking against each other as I move; it is almost as though we're going to a party, as though I'm carrying a bag full of cheap booze and we'll turn the corner to find people and noise and not the concrete platform behind the tower, dark.

The door at the back is open, as you said it was before, clanging on its hinges and we shuffle into the boiler room. As I step inside, I touch the wall and try to imagine that within a day it won't be there. It seems unmovably solid: the concrete and the litter in the corner of the room and broken glass by the window; the residual smell of cigarettes, rubbish, cannabis.

Through more doorways, torch beams hesitant before us, all of us following you until we reach the stairwell. There's trash and dried leaves on the stairs, rustling as we begin to climb. Four and a half floors up: the bag is heavy and I'm panting. There's a clunk that sounds like a bottle being kicked against a step, and Adam stumbles and yelps. The noise makes us all freeze. Heavy breathing and beyond us, quiet.

Then somewhere below us, a light comes on. It casts shadows in the stairwell: spidery lines of railings spring up the walls. Adam crouches down at once and the rest of us sink, slowly, fumbling to turn our torches off. We wait. The light downstairs stays on.

There's a thud from somewhere beneath us, and then a dog barks, twice. My face is near Diya's leg, which twitches at the sound as though someone has pinched her. Footsteps below us and a voice, echoing up to where we're crouching: 'Through here! This way!'

I inch towards the railings to look over the edge. Two boys, teenagers, with a big white dog are crossing the floor. Paint cans in hand. They've got a large, swaying lamp with them that casts these wide shadows. Rattle of ball bearings through the aerosols. Hiss of paint on the walls. Adam stands up, flicks his torch back on and begins to climb again. Below us, the boys catch sight or sound of him and shout up, 'Who's that? Who's there?' and then dash back to the exit. Footsteps receding; light fades.

When I look up you're staring at me, and smiling. 'You look so scared,' you say, and somehow it's the nicest thing you've said to me in weeks.

*

There are hundreds of videos of demolitions on the internet. Shaking cameras. Wind buffeting the speakers. A flash and then dust and the sickening lurch of the solid upright thing away from solidness, away from uprightness. Straight lines not straight anymore. Sometimes the middle of the building sinks first and the outside walls veer inwards. Sometimes it's the other way around. Sometimes there's a crowd of people who have gathered to watch, and they make 'ahs' and 'oohs' as though they're at a firework display, and then applaud.

★

We are standing inside your father's old flat. It's just you and me. The others have gone up to the top. We've brought head torches. I put mine on and toss one across to you; you grab for it but don't catch it. It rattles on the floor and the batteries roll out. You're still smiling at me as you crouch to put it back together, and it feels like a kind of heat, this shift in your mood. It hasn't been good and easy between us for so long, and now here you are, and here I am, and we are doing this thing together. You walk to a window and look down at the roundabout, the wreath of red and white car lights around it. I stand next to you for a while, long enough to notice your breaths, which are slower and deeper than mine, and to overthink what I want to say to you, so in the end I say nothing, and return to the task in hand, tipping out balloons from your bag, which you've discarded by the door, and setting up the pumps.

'Here,' I say. 'Come on. Help.'

You turn and raise a hand to shield your eyes from the beam of my torch. Your expression is vague, as though you've forgotten for a moment why we're here. Then you clear your throat and nod. You cross to me.

I watch your fingers as you fit the balloons over the pump's nozzle where the helium comes out, and then release them and knot their necks. Your hands are so busy, twisting and twisting; your face is so still.

The pumps hiss and rattle but I stop noticing after a while. We fall into a rhythm of fixing and pushing and tying and letting the balloons float up to the ceiling. I like hearing you beside me, shifting your weight on the floor, sighing; I like the glimpses of your hands at work and the way the smell of laundry detergent is just noticeable over the darker smell of the old flat. Time passes, measured out in taut grey orbs, and soon I'm not even thinking about where we are, or what we're doing, just the rising of the balloons.

*

It seems, after watching demolition videos, that there should be a way to rewind. I imagine how it would look on an old-fashioned VHS, the way the buildings would reassemble, leap upwards, soldiers caught slouching on duty. It would seem as though they'd only forgotten themselves for a moment. But on YouTube it can't look that way. I can only click backwards to the moment before the explosion and see it repeat. There's no continuity between the present and the past. You can only watch it forwards, in short bursts, and then again.

★

I'm thinking about the bath thing. I am constantly thinking about the bath thing, have been spinning out and back to it ever since, through every meeting, through every lecture, through every subsequent bath. Your breath on my breath and how quick you were to jump in. Droplet of water falling on my shoulder from a damp dagger of your hair. It's expanding in my chest and I can't seem to hold it any longer.

'Hey,' I say. 'You know that thing that happened? The bath thing?'

You don't respond. Something feels odd and I glance up. The room is crowded with balloons. They have filled the ceiling and several layers lower, so that there's only a little space around the floor that isn't full. When the beam of my head torch illuminates the grey spheres, they look translucent and murky. I extend an arm to where I guess you are; the balloons creak against each other. My hands grasp air and latex. I can't feel you. After scrabbling around I find the pump you were using. It is lying on its side on the ground.

I reach out around me and begin to feel panicked. Jostling, noisy, the balloons resemble eyes, or mouths, or eggs.

'Hello?' I say, and my voice sounds echoey. 'Are you there? I think we've done enough. I think we should find the others and go.'

The room doesn't look like a room anymore. It feels as though it is already disintegrating. Nothing is familiar; the smell, solid and damp and real when we arrived, has been replaced by the tang of the rubber.

'Hey!' I shout.

I pull my phone out of my pocket to check the time. It is 4 a.m.. I call your number and it rings through to a computerised voice saying, 'You have reached the voicemail box of' and then you saying your own name. You sound uncertain, as though you're lying. I try twice more, and then stop. Somewhere beyond the tower, sirens are wailing.

I wade through the balloons to the door, and

slide through it. They nestle on the threshold, trying to follow me out. I expect to see you in the corridor, but you aren't there, either. I text the group chat, saying I've lost you.

4.

We are sleepless and fractious and the meeting is convened around a table outside the coffee shop by the roundabout, from where we have a view of the tower. Workers are busying all over it, now, in fluorescent jackets, baubles on a tree. We're supposed to be looking at Waderley but instead I'm looking everywhere for you. Peter is here, hungover and annoyed, saying, 'Right, but where is she?' whenever I try to explain what happened – the room, the balloons, the sudden absence of you – and frowning. 'She can't miss the demolition,' he snaps, and then looks at me and says, 'Put that in the minutes, that she can't miss it,' as though that will make it true.

What I write instead is that I'm scared you are still in the tower. I write that I'm scared we left you behind, that you're stuck somehow, that you can't get out. Or: I'm scared you want to be there, that this was your plan all along. I'm scared that none of us know who you really are or were. I'm scared to check your Twitter feed in case you haven't posted since last night, and I'm scared to check your Twitter feed in case you have, are continuing to tweet, bodylessly and soundlessly from a place I can't reach. Where are you? Why won't you answer your phone?

★

Places I have not found you:

1. On the top floor of the tower, where I ran after leaving your father's flat, and saw that the others had done exactly what we, or I, had done. They'd filled a room with balloons, the same bulging grey. They had been breathing the helium to make their voices squeak, and were giggly and proud of themselves, and Kat and Adam were touching each other and kissing and whatever had been happening between them these past few weeks had finally overflowed, and nobody was really in the mood for me to panic, and they said you must have got bored and left and that it was no big deal.
2. Outside the tower on the pavement, waiting for us to emerge, smoking a cigarette.

3. On any of the streets between Waderley and our flat, walking or sitting, or waiting for a bus.
4. At home, in the bed or on the sofa, or sitting at the table, or standing in the window. Everything was as we'd left it and I could tell – it seemed clear – that you hadn't been back. In the fridge: half-eaten tray of supermarket sushi. On the floor by the front door: boots you wore to teach in, which you complained rubbed the skin of your heels. Just as it was when we left: a museum piece.
5. Here, now, inside or outside the café, waiting for us all to arrive, nursing milky coffee, thumb rolling over the screen of your phone.

★

Camera is set up on the table, pointing right at the tower, filming. Time is 10.59 and demolition is at noon and it's cold, freezing really, and the wind is making everything difficult: notebook pages fly, hair in my eyes. I sit tight and count the minutes, stretching, ballooning, into a perfectly-formed half hour, then, later, an hour. I calculate: I haven't heard your voice, haven't seen you, for

489 minutes, and I think I am falling apart.

One minute until the explosion. Peter is quivering, now, and my hands are unsteady on the keyboard. A distraction: to think of your lecture, of Ori Gersht, *the moment of destruction, the moment of creation*, the petals flying outwards towards the screen and your voice as you said, 'What is the difference between a painting, and a photograph of a painting?' Kat, Diya, Adam counting down the seconds out loud, twenty-nine, twenty-eight, twenty-seven, lurch of something in my stomach, anticipating the collapse, dropping and squirming and my lungs feel tight, as though the air we're breathing is already thick with dust, and the site around the tower is completely clear, now, nobody is allowed nearby, and there's a loud bang, just as you said there would be, and moments later a wisp of birds peels away from the roof and I'm wondering whether that would have been enough, just to film the birds taking off like that, and whether we couldn't have done something afterwards to edit it, to make it look simultaneous – the explosion and the birds – whether the Ascension of Waderley couldn't have been, after all, the kind of art that is made *from* fact, rather than the kind that *is* fact, whether a video of an explosion is as good as an explosion, better, even, because it can be rewound in a way that can't be done on YouTube or in life, eighteen, seventeen, sixteen, giving in and looking at your Twitter feed to find a single sentence posted over and over – 'When all lines are broken and no sail appears on the blank horizon, then there remains to the isolated subject in the grip of *taedium vitae* one last thing' – and hundreds of retweets and various comments along the lines of 'Have you been hacked?' but you've posted this sentence before and I remember thinking then that I understood it, but suddenly it seems to mean something else, and there's no delaying it, is there, five, four, as everyone at the table tenses and Peter says, 'Let's do this,' two, one, juts of grey smoke as though the tower has grown arms and is breaking out of itself, and the sway of the upper floors, and there they are, the balloons, astonishing, bobbing, climbing into the air, and everyone is amazed, never really thought it would work, astounded, laughing, strangers pointing and gasping, it's perfect, it's just how we imagined it, the building taking off, drifting upwards, disintegrating in the sky, weightless and speckling the clouds and all above us, now, and I'm so giddy and incredulous and buoyant that I turn to kiss you, because in all the commotion and joy I've forgotten where you aren't.

About the Authors

Kerry Andrew is a London-based composer, performer and writer. Her debut novel, *Swansong*, was published by Jonathan Cape in January 2018. She read/performed her debut short story 'One Swallow' on BBC Radio 4 in 2014. She is the winner of four British Composer Awards and has a PhD in Composition from the University of York. As a composer, she specialises in experimental vocal and choral music, music-theatre and community music. She made her BBC Proms debut in 2017 with 'No Place Like' for BBC Ten Pieces, and was 2018's BBC Young Musician Chair of the Jury. She performs alternative folk music under the banner of You Are Wolf and sings with award-winning a cappella trio Juice Vocal Ensemble.

Sarah Hall was born in Cumbria in 1974. She is the prize-winning author of five novels – *Haweswater*, *The Electric Michelangelo*, *The Carhullan Army*, *How to Paint a Dead Man* and *The Wolf Border*. Her first short story collection,

The Beautiful Indifference, won the Portico Prize and the Edge Hill Short Story Prize. The first story in the collection, 'Butchers Perfume', was shortlisted for the BBC National Short Story Award. Her second collection, *Madame Zero*, was published in 2017 and is currently shortlisted for the Edge Hill Prize. The lead story, 'Mrs Fox', won the BBC National Short Story Award, and the last story, 'Evie', was shortlisted for the Sunday Times EFG Short Story Award. 'Sudden Traveller' was commissioned by Audible for the Bard series of short stories.

Kiare Ladner's debut novel, *Nightshift*, will be published by Picador in late 2019. She wrote it together with short stories as part of a funded Creative Writing PhD at Aberystwyth University. During the PhD, her short stories were shortlisted in competitions (including the Bridport Prize, the Short Fiction Competition, the Short Sharp Stories Award and storySouth Million Writers Award). They were also published in journals and anthologies in the UK, where she lives now, and South Africa, where she grew up (these include *Lightship Anthology 1, New Contrast* and *Wasafiri*). Before the PhD, she was given the David Higham Scholarship for her MA Prose Writing at the University of East Anglia. Before that, she worked in a range of jobs for academics, with prisoners and doing nightshifts.

Born in Trinidad, **Ingrid Persaud** has had lives as a legal academic teaching at King's College London, a Goldsmith College and Central St Martins-trained visual artist and a project manager. Although she came to writing later in life, she has always been preoccupied with the power of words, both in her academic work and her exploration of text as art. Persaud is the 2017 winner of the Commonwealth Short Story Prize and her work has appeared in *Granta, Prospect* and *Pree* magazines. Her physical homes are London and Barbados which she shares with 'The Husband, teenaged twin boys, a feral chicken and two rescue dogs'.

Nell Stevens lives in London. Her memoir *Mrs Gaskell & Me* (UK) / *The Victorian and the Romantic* (US, CAN) (2018) is a blend of life writing and historical fiction about love, distance and reading. Her first book, *Bleaker House*, was published in 2017. Nell has a PhD in Victorian literature from King's College London, and an MFA in Fiction from Boston University. She is a Lecturer in Creative Writing at Goldsmiths University.

About the BBC National Short Story Award with Cambridge University

The BBC National Short Story Award is one of the most prestigious for a single short story and celebrates the best in home-grown short fiction. The ambition of the award, which is now in its thirteenth year, is to expand opportunities for British writers, readers and publishers of the short story, and honour the UK's finest exponents of the form. The award is a highly regarded feature within the literary landscape with a justified reputation for genuinely changing writers' careers.

James Lasdun secured the inaugural award in 2006 for 'An Anxious Man'. In 2012, when the Award expanded internationally for one year to mark the London Olympics, the Bulgarian writer Miroslav Penkov was victorious with his story 'East of the West'. Last year's winner was Cynan Jones for his 'exhilarating, terrifying and life-affirming' story 'The Edge of the Shoal', with previous alumni including Lionel Shriver, Zadie Smith, Hilary Mantel, Jon McGregor, Rose Tremain and William Trevor.

The winning author receives £15,000, and four further shortlisted authors £600 each. All five shortlisted stories are broadcast on BBC Radio 4 along with interviews with the writers.

In 2015, to mark the National Short Story Award's tenth anniversary, the BBC Young Writers' Award was launched in order to inspire the next generation of short story writers, to raise the profile of the form with a younger audience, and provide an outlet for their creative labours. The teenage writers shortlisted for the award have their stories featured online, and the winner's story is broadcast on BBC Radio 1. The winner of the 2017 award was 17-year-old Elizabeth Ryder for her sophisticated and original story 'The Roses'. Previous winners are Brennig Davies for 'Skinning' and Lizzie Freestone for 'Ode to a Boy Musician'.

To inspire the next generation of short story readers, teenagers around the UK are also involved in the BBC National Short Story Award via the BBC Student Critics' Award, which gives selected 16–18 year olds the opportunity to read, listen to, discuss and critique the five stories shortlisted by the judges, and have their say. The students are supported with discussion guides, teaching resources and interactions with writers and judges, for an enriching experience that brings literature to life.

The year 2018 marked the start of an exciting collaboration between the BBC and the University of Cambridge and First Story. The University of Cambridge supports all three awards, and held a short story festival at the Institute of Continuing Education, which offers a range of creative writing and English Literature programmes, in summer 2018, and curated an exclusive online exhibition of artefacts drawn from the University Library's archive to inspire and intrigue entrants of the Young Writers' Award. The charity First Story bring their experience in fostering creativity, confidence and writing skills in secondary schools serving low-income communities to bear, by supporting the Young Writers' Award and the Student Critics' Award with activity engaging young people with reading, writing and listening to short stories.

For more information on the awards, please visit www.bbc.co.uk/nssa and www.bbc.co.uk/ywa. You can also keep up-to-date on Twitter via #BBCNSSA, #BBCYWA and #shortstories

Award Partners

BBC Radio 4 is the world's biggest single commissioner of short stories, which attract more than a million listeners. Contemporary stories are broadcast every week, the majority of which are specially commissioned throughout the year. www.bbc.co.uk/radio4

BBC Radio 1 is the UK's No.1 youth station, targeting 15 to 29 year-olds with a distinctive mix of new music and programmes focusing on issues affecting young people. One of the station's key purposes is to support new British music and emerging artists, also discovering new artists through BBC Introducing. Radio 1 is also the leading voice for young people in the UK, tackling relevant issues through our documentaries, Radio 1's Life Hacks, Newsbeat as well as our social action and education campaigns. Topics covered include youth employment, sexuality, body image and bullying. BBC Radio 1 is a truly multiplatform station, enabling young audiences to connect to the network and to listen, watch

and share great content both at home and whilst on the move – via FM and DAB Radio; the BBC iPlayer Radio app; online, Freeview and other digital television platforms; and via mobile.
www.bbc.co.uk/radio1

First Story was started in 2008 by the writer William Fiennes (author of *The Music Room* and *The Snow Geese*) and former teacher Katie Waldegrave (author of *The Poets' Daughters*) with the mission of changing lives through writing. First Story exists to bring talented, professional writers into secondary schools serving low-income communities to work with teachers and students to foster confidence, creativity and writing skills. Since 2008, First Story has run almost 400 residencies in schools, given 8,000 students the chance to take part in weekly creative writing workshops, worked with 400 acclaimed authors and 500 teachers and librarians, published almost 400 anthologies, and enabled over 140,000 pieces of original student writing.
www.firststory.org.uk

The mission of the **University of Cambridge** is to contribute to society through the pursuit of education, learning and research at the highest international levels of excellence. To date, 96 affiliates of the University have won the Nobel Prize. Founded in 1209, the University comprises 31 autonomous Colleges, which admit students and provide small-group tuition, and 150 departments, faculties and institutions. Cambridge is a global university. Its 19,000 student body includes 3,700 international students from 120 countries. Cambridge researchers collaborate with colleagues worldwide, and the University has established larger-scale partnerships in Europe, Asia, Africa and America. The BBC National Short Story Award is being supported by the School of Arts and Humanities, Faculty of English, University Library and the new University of Cambridge Centre for Creative Writing which is part of the University of Cambridge Institute of Continuing Education, which provides courses to members of the public.

www.cam.ac.uk/bbcshortstory